MW01199348

Hardy Haul
At Hardy Hall

The First Teddy Quillfeather Mystery

Hardy Haul at Hardy Hall

CHAPTER ONE

*In which timing is everything, all hope is lost for the next generation,
a burglary is announced, and Teddy Quillfeather prepares for what
promises to be a challenging away derby.*

The key to a successful heist, almost anyone who's ever heisted
successfully will tell you, is timing. There's a chap in Brighton,
known to the police as Jimmy Elbows, who'll tell you that the key is
bribing the security guards, but Jimmy Elbows has no imagination at
all and every year at Christmas, in lieu of a unique and considered
gift, he renews his mother's subscription to *Safe and Lockbox,* a
periodical she doesn't read.

For everyone else, the scheme must be simple but sophisticated,
flexible but fastidious, and above all it must be executed with the
precision timing of a Swiss watchmaker taking a meeting with his
accountant.

Taking an example closer to hand, the perfect pinch is an
aggregation of overlapping subtleties, meticulously performed by all
parties, including oblivious bystanders, such as the heist which was
unfolding at 11:02 PM precisely, on a cold, crisp, calm winter's eve
outside one of London's oldest and richest institutions.

The guards, far from being bribed or, for that matter, corruptible
(so much for the best laid plans of Jimmy Elbows), were on alert.
They had been warned by police that their charge was targeted by
known masters of the swift shift. These heroes are Jack 'Daw'
MacGraw and Donny 'Noddy' Wandle. Daw, the older and wiser and
wider of the two, was a retired constable making up his monthly
means, shortened by a son-in-law who still struggled to establish
himself as an abstract landscape artist. Noddy, tall and thin and
swaddled in his uniform, was, during the day, Latin master at a
school for girls. In short, both men were hardened cynics and neither
was anyone's fool.

So, as they held their positions outside the high columned gates, beneath a flickering gaslight, stamping just enough to keep the circulation primed for the chase, they received the girl who approached them with a sort of bemused condescension.

"I say…" The girl was perhaps fourteen years old, in kneesocks, plaits and woollens, and wearing her hair in braids. Noddy, in particular, was on a keen edge of vigilance. "There are some people climbing over the wall around that corner."

"You don't say." Daw spoke with a wink in his voice. "A criminal gang, is it?"

"I don't know about that," acknowledged the girl. "Just a couple of people climbing over the wall from the top of a hansom cab."

"And I suppose you'd like us to leave our post and go and have a look, would you?" asked Noddy with that soupçon of irony that he believed, inaccurately, made him such a respected Latin master.

"Suit yourself." In that instant a horse whinnied, a branch broke, an 'oof' was uttered from somewhere in the chill, still fog. "I'm only telling you — there are some people climbing over the wall. I thought it'd be the sort of thing to interest you."

"And so it is," Daw assured her. "You've done your best, and it's all very convincing, but next time you might either create a distraction or send a decoy. Not both."

"Rather gives the game away," added Noddy, with an avuncular, advisory tone.

The girl shrugged and turned away and disappeared into the night. Noddy and Daw smiled clubbishly at each other. Noddy rolled his eyes. The silence, if any such thing was needed, confirmed their reasoning.

But then, from behind the very gates, somewhere on the grounds, came a squawk.

"A bird," judged Daw who, as mentioned, was a man of the world.

Another sound followed.

"Was that a bird, Daw?" asked Noddy.

"No," resolved Daw. "That was giggling."

Impossibly, someone had got past them, and was even now on the grounds. Daw pulled the keys from his pocket, dropped them, recovered them, and before a minute had passed since the first positive identification of giggling, he had unlocked the gate and the two security guards were hurrying — in low, zig-zagging movements, in the fashion of the Royal Fusiliers — into the darkness and mist.

The giggling was moving and intermittently accompanied by a splash and a clang, two 'shushes' and a bang. The grounds were shadowless in the grey gloom of a hazy new moon and Daw and Noddy could only follow by sound and seasoned instincts. By and by, the giggling stopped, and Daw and Noddy were back at the gates, beyond which a hansom cab was just clopping out onto the shiny cobblestones.

"Halt!" ordered Daw, and he and Noddy pushed themselves against the unyielding gates. They had left them unlocked — in retrospect something they might not do should similar circumstances arise in future — but now they wouldn't open. Wedged underneath on the outside was a two-tone leather T-strap pump, medium heel, size seven.

All the guards could do was watch the black satin carriage fade into the night from behind the bars and beneath the sign of one of London's oldest and richest institutions, The London Zoo.

❧

"But wait!" urged Elmer Clarence Piptree III, with the authority of master of ceremonies and wealthiest toff in a ballroom filled to the rafters with the tuxedoed and sequinned deco generation of London's listed families. "With only…" Elmer withdrew his pocket watch and stared hard at it, "…some time remaining before midnight, Team

Teddy and Freddy outright win the Chelsea and Mayfair Ample Merriweather Memorial Scavenger Hunt, 1928, with one hundred and eighty points, including ten points for an off-menu omelette from the Ritz, twenty points for a police whistle, and a honking great one hundred and fifty points for the hunt's only entry of a live penguin."

Theodora 'Teddy' Quillfeather and Frederica 'Freddy' Hannibal-Pool hopped up onto the stage with Elmer. Freddy required assistance, because she wore only one shoe, and the penguin had to be carried, because he was a penguin. Apart from the footwear shortcoming, Teddy and Freddy were fully flappered in sack dresses and feather fascinators and both were constructed to distract. Freddy was the taller and blonder and Teddy monopolised all the brunette bob the pair had to share.

"Tip top, Teddy," congratulated Elmer. "Stellar scavenging again this year. Where did you get Tuxedo Bird?"

"At the Cricketers," claimed Teddy. "He was playing darts and, as you might imagine, losing badly. What do we win?"

"A bottle of champagne."

"Right oh. Where is it?"

"Oh, pffff," dismissed Elmer. "Long gone. I can offer you this lovely penguin."

"Talking of penguins, Tedds," Freddy talked casually of penguins, "we should probably be getting this one back to his tribe."

The penguin, conversely, expressed no such urgency. He had found the basin of melted ice in which hundreds of bottles of Bollingers had prepared to meet their fates with cool equanimity, and which still contained a half a tin of black beluga caviar.

"Can you manage, Freddy?" asked Teddy. "I'm meant to be in Kent tomorrow. Place called Hardy Hall."

"Topsy Turville's pile of rocks?"

"That's it. Know it?"

4

"I should say so," said Freddy. "All the very latest in country house comforts. Tommy Lord Turville bought the lot on the spot for Lady Turville on speculation of great things — they say that he's developed a secret formula for a super glue called Stickle."

"Is a secret formula for a super glue something that buys country houses?"

"It is if it remains a secret until it's brought to market," said Freddy. "And provided it's properly super. They say that Stickle can repair the wing of an aeroplane, mid-flight."

"Well, finally," enthused Teddy. "I can't tell you how often I've been on planes when the wing has fallen off."

"The real money is in the domestic market, as I understand it. Putting your antique bisque back together before the parents get home, that sort of thing. It's said to be completely invisible."

"It'll have to be an improvement over nail polish and denial," said Teddy. "What's Hardy Hall like?"

"It's all right, actually. Positively seething with opportunity for right-minded villainy. For one thing, it's on an island and it's got a moat, so it's effectively an island on a pond on an island on a pond. It's got a working cannon on the roof and a dumb waiter. Oh, and don't forget, the drain pipe on the west wall is absolutely not to be trusted."

"Noted."

"One of your mother's ultimatums?"

"It is," confirmed Teddy. "There are no less than three first born beneficiaries there this weekend. Mama's hoping that proximity to one of them will cause me to sprout grandchildren."

"Dire," Freddy called it. "I hope I can count on you to behave abominably."

"You know me, Fredds."

"Then what can go wrong?"

"I'll let you know."

Hardy Hall, if asked, would probably say that it prefers to be described as a castle. It most certainly was a castle, once, when the little island of Hardy Holm was first settled in the thirteenth century and the local peasants were casting about for a feudal lord to whom they could give half their wheat and wool.

Times being what they were, the original castles were knocked down and seiged and burned and pulled apart to construct a local church and mill. Each time it was built back stronger and sillier until, today, it has a perfectly square moat right up to the edges of the exterior walls, themselves composed of four square towers topped with ramparts and connected by residential halls, all surrounding an interior courtyard of fountains and flowers.

The grounds are the tailored shrubbery, weeping elms, beech tree bowers, wild English gardens of mint and rose, a trapezoid yew maze, and the scattered chantries and blothies and sheds occupying the island, all looking quite scant and slightly embarrassed in their winter minimum.

The drawbridge was long ago replaced by a permanent stone bridge that does no tricks at all, but is well capable of supporting the weight of a 1927 4.5 litre Invicta, even the candy-apple red model, which features a steamer trunk strapped to the rack and a heavily-sequined flapper behind the wheel.

Teddy tooted as she tooled beneath the beech canopy and across the bridge and into the courtyard where she stopped the engine so that she could hear herself whistle in admiration at what can be done with a little stone and ivy and six hundred years of accumulated charm.

"Theodora!" On the steps of the entrance — a grand granite and glass opus at the effective back of the courtyard — was Lady Gladys

Turville and a footman. It was Lady Turville, Teddy reasoned, who had just called her by name.

"What ho, Glitz." Teddy tipped out of the two-seater, in the style of the time, without opening the door, and the ladies crunched across the gravel into a sororal embrace. Lady Gladys was the age of Teddy's mother, within a stretched decade, but had no children of her own and had been anticipating a good, solid meddle in her friend's daughter's life the way a child looks forward to Christmas.

"How was the drive down?" Lady Gladys — Glitz to anyone who also knows Teddy — was a well-preserved woman the way Hardy Hall was a well-preserved castle; not young but somehow the better for it, and unafraid to wear her wealth on her sleeve, not to mention around her neck, on her head, hanging from her ears and pinned to her lacy bodice, often more than once.

"Lovely day for it." Teddy gave a referential deferential to the cornflower-coloured sky above. "But all the way here I kept hearing 'go back to London!'"

"Oh, dear, whoever would say such a thing?"

"Well, me mainly, I talk to myself when I drive alone, but I soldiered on."

"You'll be glad you did." Glitz slid her arm into Teddy's and guided her towards the house. "Do you even know who's here — Beauregard Pilewright."

"Not really!"

"Yes!"

"I can absolutely not believe it," marvelled Teddy. "Who's Beauregard Pilewright?"

"Do you not read the society pages, Teddy?"

"Not much I don't, no," confided Teddy. "They're always saying such terrible truths about me. Really, there ought to be a law."

"Beauregard Pilewright is only one of London's most desirable properties," peddled Glitz. "They say that he must marry before he's thirty to collect his inheritance."

"How old is he now?"

"Twenty-nine."

"Ish," expressed Teddy with signature nuance. "He must have a face like a boiled bladder."

"He's a very handsome young man," insisted Glitz.

"Right, well, just in case I'm unable to hold down my hors d'oeuvres, who else is on the menu?"

"Tilden Stollery."

"Stilts," checked Teddy. "I know him well. Lovely chap. Taller than me by about six hands and a hat, but he's just the man to know when the sun's coming up and you're running out of Bollinger's. What's he doing here, though?"

"Well, Teddy, your mother hoped…"

"No, no, I know the rules and play of Bachelor Bingo, goodness knows I've played it often enough, but I mean what's he doing here in Kent — he's proposed to me a dozen times at least this year alone from the convenience of Mayfair, close to good schools and shops and with reliable transport links."

"He's heir to a diamond mine."

"I know he is. He's drowning in dosh. Comes all the way up to his ankles."

"And then there's Algernon Brookbridge," Lady Gladys completed the inventory.

"Algy?"

"You know him?"

"Nope," said Teddy. "Just wondering what his parents were thinking."

"His father is Abernathy Brookbridge."

"So you're saying it's revenge."

"Of Brookbridge Industrial Adhesives," clarified Glitz. "They're very successful…" Lady Gladys lowered her voice the way people do when they're conveying important information they, themselves, do not understand. "…and a most vital business alliance of Tom's," by whom she meant her husband, Thomas Lord Turville.

Teddy paused the journey on the steps. "Is that the lot?"

"It is," said Glitz. "And any girl would be lucky to have any one of them."

"Let us first put them to the test," proposed Teddy. "I find that the best measure of a man's character is how he responds to rejection."

"Teddy…" Lady Gladys crossed her arms in a manner carefully calculated to display her diamond owl brooch with jade eyes. "You should know that your mother and I have spoken, and she's very anxious to see you start your own family."

"No kidding?" asked Teddy. "She should probably mention it two or three times a day."

"She means it, Teddy. She's authorised me to tell you that if you haven't reached an understanding with one of these gentlemen by the end of the weekend she's selling your car."

"Vicky?" Teddy looked back at her candy-apple Invicta.

"And the flat in Mayfair."

"So she can buy me a new one in Chelsea?"

"Teddy, you'll find a husband this weekend or your mother says you'll be moving back home to Berkshire."

The last time that Teddy had been caught speechless was when she fell out of a tree on the grounds of the London Zoo, and even then she'd managed a comparatively eloquent 'oof'. Now, she could only gaze at Vicky the fussy four litre and try and fail to focus.

"Right oh," she finally said with the appearance of capitulation. "Anybody else on hand this weekend? Any axe murderers?"

"Sir Oswald and Lady Woolpit are here, and Major Lonegrave," inventoried Glitz, "and Portia Beanfield."

"Portion is here?" perked Teddy. "Which of us is second prize?"

"Portia is just visiting while her flat is being redecorated." Glitz scanned the courtyard for spies and lowered her voice. "She has a young man in London."

"Perhaps she'd like one in Kent, too," suggested Teddy. "Any track or trace of Aunty Azalea? Mama said that she was sending her down on a spying mission."

"Your Aunt Azalea is here as chaperone, Teddy."

"That is, essentially, what I said," said Teddy. "She's here then, is she?"

"It's hard to say with any certainty," mulled Glitz. "You know that Azalea likes to keep as much to herself as possible."

"I'll say," agreed Teddy. "I was up at her place in Hertfordshire last summer for a week while my photo was circulated amongst the bluebottles of the metropolis. I only saw her the one time I opened a broom closet while looking for a stout rope. She claimed that she was sorting out the brooms but, really, who sorts brooms? In any case, there was just the one broom."

The ladies were now in the entrance hall which, like many such foyers retrofitted into castles that had been designed chiefly for self-defence, was a low, dark, oak-panelled tunnel leading to promising things — heavy great hardwood doors lined its walls and another hall intersected it, and at the far end, lit from all directions like the apse of a cathedral on a sunny day, a wood and brass staircase wound up and away and into the unknown.

Glitz jostled a rope bellpull and then stood back, with her hands on her hips, and considered Teddy with a critical eye, as though the dim lighting of the hall exposed heretofore unnoticed scars and tattoos.

"Have you brought anything to wear?"

"Oh, sure," dismissed Teddy with a wave. "I've got my old hockey uniform and a bear costume in which, even if it's me saying so, I'm quite fetching."

"I mean jewellery," scolded Glitz. "Boys are drawn to shiny things. It's in their nature. It's something to do with poor night vision, I think."

"Doubtless."

"I'll loan you something."

Glitz spoke with the impatient camaraderie of the enthusiast, eager to show off her collection to a captive audience. Nevertheless Teddy, who had been heroically resisting more than a glance at it, now dropped her eyes to the complex netting of gold and green hanging around the neck of her hostess. Glitz followed her gaze.

"Do you like it?" she asked. "I designed it myself."

It was, in fact, the ugliest necklace that Teddy had ever seen, but Lady Gladys, by her own admission, had designed it herself, and honeyed words were called for.

"That's the ugliest necklace I've ever seen."

"Not really." Glitz posed in a hall mirror.

"Actually, no, it isn't," admitted Teddy. "Once, at the V&A, I saw a necklace formed of igneous boulders and anchor chain. I think it was designed to cause the drowning of a sacrificial elephant. That might have been uglier."

"I know..." Glitz tried a different angle. "It looked well enough on paper. You wouldn't have thought designing jewellery would turn out to be so specialised, would you?"

"Yes."

"Not a word to Tom," admonished Glitz. "It cost a fortune. He hates it, too, but I've convinced him that he's just a boor."

"Why, Glitz, you're quite devious for a simple designer of hideous jewellery, aren't you?"

"Oh, that was easy," said Glitz. "He thinks everybody else likes opera, too." Glitz looked down at the thing. It was a sort of geometric latticework housing rectangular green emeralds placed, by the most charitable analysis, randomly, and descending to a pendant of jade the size of a golf ball. It looked, more than anything else, like a New York skyscraper with most of the windows shot out. "Anyway, he wants to lock it up in his safe this weekend."

"That's probably best for all concerned."

"No…" Glitz assumed a wide-eyed earnestness, like a squirrel remembering an appointment. "He's convinced that, at some point this weekend, there's going to be a heist."

CHAPTER TWO

Which features the difficulties inherent in the amateur design of jewellery and penguins.

Midgeham had been a member of staff at Hardy Hall for most of his life, starting as the boot and knife boy and, by quality of character and commitment and, yes, sometimes pure luck, he climbed the ranks of domestic service to second footman, footman, main floor butler, chauffeur for a brief and disastrous afternoon, main floor butler again, and then butler and head of staff. His was a calm, comfortable correctness — he knew that he was right or, were he not, he was assumed to be by those who regard career butlers as unimpeachable authorities on all matters of dress and decorum and dining and what else, after all, is there?

Midgeham carefully cultivated the aesthetic, too. He had seven identical morning suits and at any time at least three of them were pressed and poised to see action, he maintained a slim figure to meet the expectations of those who assume, if they ever thought about it, that butlers don't eat, and he had assiduously lost all the hair on the top of his head in his mid-forties. He spoke as one suffering severe nasal congestion, which he never did, and he addressed everyone as though he was doing so from beneath the brim of a low hat. He never lost his nerve and to him all matters were household matters, from a dripping faucet to a death in the family.

And so, when he approached Lady Gladys in the drawing room before dinner and said, "There is a penguin in the moat, madame," his delivery was tonally identical to, for instance, that morning when he announced that the bacon would be late.

"That's mine." Teddy raised a hand. "It's why I had Midgeham move me to the ground floor, by the way, so Tuxedo Bird can come and go via the balcony."

"Where did you get a penguin?" asked Glitz.

"Just outside Wrotham," said Teddy. "His car broke down."

"Will he be staying long?"

"Just the weekend. I was meant to drop him off at the zoo this morning but for some reason they're operating with increased security."

Introductions had already been made, but everyone was present for this exchange, offering a good opportunity for a quick roll call and to put the players on the board.

"Doubtless the increased security was for an auspicious visitor. They must have known you were coming." *Beauregard Pilewright. Described previously and accurately as 'very handsome', with high cheekbones and chestnut hair impeccably shaved and shorn, and smartly turned out in swallowtails and stiff shirtfront and a bowtie that looked like it had been tied by a team of top physicists. He stood by the fire, gazing across the room at himself in the mirror.*

"What is a penguin, exactly?" *Lady Mildred Woolpit. Middle-brow, middle-class, middle-aged, middle-school friend of Lady Gladys. Emerald-green evening gown about which she was self-conscious.*

"It's a sort of fish, darling, with feathers." *Sir Oswald Woolpit. Jowelly. Inflated and unbalanced moustache. Bowtie; same. Emerald-green dinner jacket to which he was indifferent. Sat next to his wife beneath the mirror.*

"Shall I take it back to the zoo for you Teddy? Only too chuffed to be of use, you know. We could go together, if you like, and then have lunch at Barribault's and after go to Antibes and get sort of married, as it were." *Tilden 'Stilts' Stollery. Gaunt, in the manner of a vulture or ship's mast. Black silk swallowtails for which he had kept a team of tailors on retainer for a year. Occupying the corner furthest from the chandelier.*

"You haven't really got a penguin, Teddy. Can it sleep in my room tonight?" *Portia 'Portion' Beanfield. Often compared favourably to a bug in a rug. Metallic-gold sack dress. Not wearing her glasses, which she needs to see. Wearing high heels, which she needs to see over things. Standing next to Stilts, creating unfortunate juxtaposition for both parties.*

"Are penguins not made up sort of things, like kangaroos? Or goldfish?" *Algernon Brookbridge. Hair like a haystack in a storm. Built for rugby. Not built for the tuxedo he was wearing. Holding position beneath a painting long-assumed to depict a Turville antecedent's contribution to victory at Agincourt, facing the garden doors.*

"Kangaroos are all too real, young man. Devilish clever, too. Mob of them once in Yulara made off with our horses. Ransomed them back to us for all our food." *Major Stanley Lonegrave.* "And then we had no food. Had to eat the horses." *Ageless as the empire, but physically mid-sixties. Military bearing. Believed himself to be well turned out in a bowtie with a safari jacket. Wasn't.*

"A fully-grown adult male Emperor Penguin can eat up to six pounds of fish per day, so if he stays more than three days we'll need to restock the pike in the moat." *Thomas Lord Turville. Typical in size and colouring of the common or garden English industrial tycoon — big and broad in bespoke black and whites, appears to be constantly calculating huge sums in his head. Smoking his pipe by the French doors which he had opened as the single accommodation of Lady Turville's expressed preference that he not smoke that pipe indoors and in company.* "Is it a fully-grown male Emperor Penguin, Midgeham?"

"I was unable to form an opinion, m'lord," owned up Midgeham, which brings the census full circle. The butler, to complete the staging, wasn't anywhere for very long, as he was moving about with a tray of champagne cocktails.

"You know, Theodora," Beau Pilewright tore himself away from his reflection and shone his light on Teddy, "you're even more beautiful than your pictures in the paper."

"I should hope so," fretted Teddy. "Last time my photo was in the rags I hadn't slept in two days and I was wearing a tinsel wig.

Really, I don't even know what *The Times* was thinking, sending a photographer to Baron Boxgrove's funeral."

Beau smiled indulgently and some fleeting source of light, undetectable under normal conditions, glittered off his teeth.

"You're joking, of course."

"Okay."

"I refer to the photograph of you and your father at the groundbreaking ceremony for the hospital he's endowing in Berkshire," beamed Beau.

"Dear Papa," sighed Teddy. "He does like to have his ground broken." She leaned to within whispering distance of Beauregard. "Between you and me, it's nothing to do with hospitals and railway stations — he's looking for the tomb of Ozymandias."

"In Berkshire?"

"I know," lamented Teddy. "Some say madness runs in my family, but that's a clear exaggeration — it's much more like a leisurely walk with occasional bursts of speed."

Beauregard smiled once again that indulgent smile that some — Teddy for instance — might call condescending. He also flicked an imaginary speck of dust from his sleeve.

"I, too, have enjoyed considerable good fortune in the markets."

"You must tell me where you go," said Teddy. "I feel I'm always overpaying for eggs."

"I mean the financial markets," clarified Beau. "But what a fool I am, talking about my absurdly successful stock portfolio to a beautiful woman on such a night as this. There is a tide in the affairs of men which, taken at the flood, leads on to fortune."

"Julius Caesar."

"And she knows her Shakespeare," swooned Beau. "Then I hope you take my meaning."

"You think it's going to rain?"

"My fondest ambition is that you might allow me to accompany you after dinner for a walk in the garden."

"That was going to be my next guess." Teddy swallowed her coupe of champagne in a single bottoms-up and took another from Midgeham's tray. "I'll pencil you in on the prance card, Bobo, but I make no guarantees. I drove down from London this afternoon and was very much looking forward to a quiet evening in, picking gnats out of my teeth."

During this exchange, Teddy had been casting about the room for distractions and repeatedly made eye contact with Stilts. It was an easy mistake to make. There's something morbidly magnetic about a chap staring, and Stilts had added the allure of an eager, imploring smile from the top of a mast, like an ingratiating wind sock. He gave the effect of being everywhere at once, and even when Teddy set her gaze on the garden he appeared in the reflection of the French doors, now scrunching up his face and waving. She waved back, very much in the spirit of Macbeth's advisory *'If it were done when 'tis done, then 'twere well 'twere done quickly.'* Stilts galloped over and Beauregard returned to mirror duty.

"What ho, Stilts," greeted Teddy. "You're here and all."

"I am," agreed Stilts. "Your mother asked Lady Gladys to ask my mother to send me down."

"How spontaneous and romantic."

"Isn't it just?" Stilts swirled his cocktail as, no doubt, he'd seen Beauregard do with such aplomb, and created a whirlpool that caused the champagne to overflow its banks onto his sleeve. "Oh."

Stilts gazed down on Teddy with the big, hopeful eyes of a doleful soul, like a friendless giraffe. Teddy chose her words accordingly, in the key of kindness.

"But, you doddering great hazard to flight, don't you get enough of being thrown over in London?"

"Your mother gave my mother to understand that you might have a change of heart this weekend," said Stilts with earnest enthusiasm. "I wanted to be on hand, in case that were so."

"Oh, I see." Teddy drew inspiration from her champagne. "Well, in point of fact, she may well be right, Stilts, but don't you see that I've only been trying to protect you."

"I'm a big boy, as it were, don't you know."

"And how," agreed Teddy. "But I wasn't protecting you from rejection, but from the curse."

"Curse?"

"Well, call it an uncanny trend, if you want to steer clear of hyperbole," considered Teddy. "Might just be a coincidence that every chap I've ever agreed to marry has died under strange circumstances."

"Really?"

"Twelve isn't that many, after all, is it?"

"Twelve chaps?"

"Mmm-hm." Teddy held up a closed hand and counted off with her fingers. "Poisoning, poisoning, electric tram, fell out a window, poisoning again..." she closed her hand to bank the first five, "...pushed off Westminster Bridge, electrocution, gas explosion, locked in a coal cellar for an entire summer, fell backwards onto a pitchfork..."

"Just a tick — who pushed the chap off Westminster Bridge?"

"No one. He fell."

"You just now said that he was pushed."

"He fell, Stilts." Teddy regarded him from beneath hooded eyes. "I stand by that."

"If you were to accept me, Teddy, I would die a happy man, as it were."

"Yish." Teddy took an exasperated draw on her champagne. "You really should put this capacity for commitment to a more achievable cause, Stilts. World peace? Are you interested in world peace? No? Very well, then, like the other candidates you'll have a chance to defend your proposals to the board of trustees at some point this weekend. I'm in a position to offer you the coveted post-luncheon slot, when I'm slow and dull with meat and mead."

"I'll take it, as it were."

"Right oh." Teddy framed these as parting words and sidled subtly away, cocktail-party fashion. "You can take me for a row on the pond, weather permitting."

Teddy's intention had been to catch up with Portion, who was now standing alone in a neutral corner, but as she passed Algernon Brookbridge she was struck by his absence of expression. He gazed idly and vacantly out the French doors and into the darkness. Teddy followed his line of vision to see that he was, in fact, staring off into space.

"Oh, what ho, Teddy." Algy snapped back to reality. "Can I see your penguin?"

"Are you not going to take a crack at charming me into a thin paste?"

"Is that a prerequisite for seeing the penguin?"

"You'd think so, going by the performances I've encountered so far. Oh, thank you, Midgeham." Teddy retrieved two more champagne cocktails from the passing tray. "Did your mother not explain the rules?"

Algy, who, as mentioned, is constructed in a manner mainly influenced by the school of thought that dictates that a young man should look as much like a bus as is practicable, fiddled with the button of his dinner jacket, which was too small to actually meet at the front.

"Yes." Algy proved a most adept button-fiddler. "She said that I'm to be bright and fascinating, and I'm to press upon you the importance of an alliance between our families."

"Are you quite sure she meant me?"

"Oh, yes, quite sure." Algy nodded with a confidence that in the next moment vanished like smoke on the wind. "Didn't she?"

"Well, I don't know, for certain." Teddy knotted her brow in reflection. "I mean to say, all this talk of my family. It makes me wonder."

"Wonder what?"

"Just what she might mean. I have no family, to speak of, unless you count Lord and Lady Turville, who are kind enough to let me visit once a year. And of course the parish."

"The parish?"

"Bermondsey and Lambeth," elucidated Teddy. "Essentially my family. I don't know what I'd do without them."

"Just a minute, you don't have parents?"

"It's very painful for me to talk about, Algy."

"I'm sorry."

"They were both killed in two separate ballooning accidents."

"What an extraordinary coincidence."

"Not really," said Teddy. "They were each trying to set a record for crossing the channel in a hot air balloon."

"And now you just have…"

"The parish," completed Teddy. "That's right. I rely on them for everything — shelter, food, petrol for the Invicta…"

"No, I mean to say, your parents left you nothing?"

"They spent almost everything we had on those balloons," grieved Teddy. "The rest they had with them."

"It's a wonder my mother didn't know all this."

"It's only just happened," said Teddy. "It's why the memory is still so raw."

"Of course. Quite so." Algy spoke like a man called to order. "Sorry."

"So if you want to tell your mother that you gave it your honest best but I just didn't measure up to the Brookbridge minimum specifications, I'll back you up."

"Oh, I say, dash it, no." Algy was, even before a scrum half and a voting member of the Rugby Football Union, a gentleman. "You don't suppose all that matters to me, do you?"

"I was rather counting on it, yes."

"Well it dashed well doesn't," insisted Algy. "Teddy, please do me the honour of accompanying me on a tour of the grounds this evening."

"Can't do this evening, I'm afraid," said Teddy. "I can tentatively schedule you for tomorrow after tea, but you'll be happy to know that this coincides with when I exercise Tuxedo Bird."

"Is that the penguin?"

"It is."

"Done."

"Right oh. Now, I'm just going to catch up with an old friend, if you'll excuse me." Teddy slipped away on the current of closing comments and drifted into the corner with Portion.

"What ho, Ports," greeted Teddy. "Not drinking? These champer dampers are lovely."

"Is that Teddy?"

"The same. Do you want to feel my face?"

"I recognise the voice." Portion nodded happily. "I've put my drink down and now I can't find it."

"It's next to you on the mantelpiece."

Portion stared hard left.

"Other side," coached Teddy.

"Oh, there it is. Thanks Tedds."

"Why don't you just wear your specs?"

"You know what a weed I feel wearing them in public." Portion seized her glass in both hands and held it to her lips.

"Not half the weed you'll feel when you fall into the moat." Teddy stepped back for a broader view. "How high are those heels? You come up almost to my shoulders."

"I'm not sure." Portion glanced down at her feet as though just that moment noticing that she was wearing shoes. "Two inches? It's hard to know — they're French."

"Oh, French, of course," said Teddy. "And, famously, a French inch is equivalent to the breadth of a cobbler's fist. You fall from that height, Portion, and you'll do yourself an injury. What are you doing down here, anyway, at the pitch of London's primary party season?"

"Well, then, what are you doing here?"

"A daughter's duty." Teddy gestured — pointlessly, for Portion couldn't see it — at the field of play. "Mama says I must find a way of repelling this lot by the end of the weekend. That's not precisely what she said, but it's how I interpret the role."

"And there we go," said Portion. "I thought you might need someone to help set something on fire, in light of your views on settling down."

"I'm just being fair to all the other blokes," confirmed Teddy. "Altruistic, I call it."

Midgeham, who had popped out and back into existence in that discreet way of butlers and oriental assassins, circulated another tray of coupes and said to Lord Turville, "Dinner will be served shortly, m'lord. You wished to be reminded."

"Quite right, Midgeham." Lord Turville knocked out his pipe on the step loudly and elaborately and then said to Her Ladyship, "Hand it over, Gladdy."

"So soon?"

"It's been dark for hours," seemingly non sequitured her husband, but then Glitz made a show of reluctantly removing her ugly green necklace and flowing it into his hand. He marched through the door next to the mirror, and on no less than three occasions put his head back into the room to, by all appearances, confirm that he wasn't being followed. Presently he rejoined the party and closed the door behind him. "Safe now," he announced.

"Theodora." In the interim, Lady Dorothea Woolpit and her husband had formed an offensive line. "I understand that you may have a big announcement to make this weekend." Lady Woolpit spoke in that teasy, breezy way of the vocational gossip. "You know that Babbette Middlingport's daughter Melany got engaged at New Year's to Chester Wideacre, who they say spent a summer in Paris studying figure drawing, and came home with a beard." Lady Dora managed to expel 'Paris', 'figure drawing' and 'beard' with the same whisper of high scandal. "It didn't take, of course. When they met again at the engagement party they didn't recognise one another."

"I know," reminisced Teddy. "It was possibly the best New Year's party ever. Certainly the longest. The police were still making arrests on the second Sunday of Epiphany."

"It's for the best," confided Lady Dora. "They say Chester's an anarchist."

"He was," clarified Teddy. "For about a weekend, until he learned that they don't have dinner parties or yachts."

"What is an anarchist, when it comes to it?" asked Lady Dora.

"It's a chap who doesn't eat meat of any kind," replied Sir Oswald with trademark confidence.

"Like Cylia Vale's boy, Tewkesbury." Dora presented this fresh connection like a costermonger breaking open a particularly juicy pineapple. "Cylia sent him to school in Geneva for a year after he settled two breach of promise suits in a row — with the same girl. Well, I don't like to talk, but I hear he came home an anarchist."

"Atheist," corrected Sir Oswald. "He came back an atheist."

"And what's an atheist?" Dora allowed her impatience with this deluge of obscure human fancies to slip into her tone.

"Ah." Sir Oswald, who enjoyed exercising his economy of facts in company, was having a bumper night. "An atheist is a chap who doesn't go in for modern art. Opposite of an aesthete."

"Modern art."

"You know, all those shapes and smears that are meant to be ladies bathing."

"Oh dear."

"That's right," confirmed Teddy. "I think it extends to all the arts, now."

"That's correct, young Teddy," approved Oswald. "Few atheists regard any poet after Keats worthy of the title."

"I think I might be an atheist," declared Lady Dora.

"Oh, I can tell you I certainly am," Teddy assured her. "My whole family are staunch atheists. Mother especially. And our vicar."

"Well, yes, of course," said Oswald. "One would expect no less from a member of the clergy."

"Talking of church, Teddy," Dora cast her eyes over the three suitors, "have you formed an early preference? I won't tell a soul."

"I'm still trialling approaches," Teddy replied like a team manager doing a match-side interview. "They're all showing remarkable endurance."

"Mister Pilewright does very well in the City," reported Dora. "They say he's a positive typhoon."

"Tycoon, dear," corrected Oswald. "A species of rodent, prized in North America for its fur."

"And terribly, terribly charming," continued Dora. "We had him up at Hollows for the start of grouse season. You remember Oswald…"

Oswald remembered, and said so, "It was when we had the robbery."

"That's right…" enthused Dora. "There was a heist."

"A heist?" repeated Teddy.

"Major Lonegrave was there too, wasn't he darling?" asked Dora.

"And Algy Brookbridge," sir Oswald saw and raised.

"Brookbridge Industrial Adhesives," Dora translated for relevance. "And of course, you know that Mister Stollery's family makes their fortune in precious stones."

And with that the players and the programme were in position for what happened next, except that what happened next was that Midgeham banged the dinner gong.

❦

At about four o'clock the next morning something awoke Tuxedo Bird, who had always been a light sleeper but particularly so when travelling. He blinked at the blackness beyond the balcony windows of Teddy's room, wherein he had been sleeping in a picnic basket lined with dozens of knitting and crocheting projects that Lady Gladys had begun and abandoned, and he saw that a light snow was falling. Little white sprites danced against the void of night, enjoying a brief and carefree existence before dissolving on the surface of the moat, and Tuxedo Bird thought of home.

Had he not gone straight back to sleep and instead investigated whatever it was that had woken him, he might have seen a shadowy figure disappearing out the bedroom door. Had he, furthermore, hopped out of the basket and out the door and down the north hall and then turned left at the west hall and continued to the drawing room and (had he been able to open the door) gone in and continued to the office of Lord Turville (the door of which would have presented yet another practical obstacle to this hypothetical) he

25

would have seen there, in the grey glow of encompassing winter night, a most extraordinary thing; the wall safe of Thomas Lord Turville was open and it was empty.

CHAPTER THREE

In which the rules of decorum of the English country manor are flouted in the observation, and the blistering pace of technology claims another victim.

"Good morning, Teddy dear. Did you steal my necklace last night?"

Glitz was speaking freely because she and Teddy were alone in the second dining room. Lady Gladys was at the buffet, energetically agitating her homemade forest berry jam, which had separated. She was in a velvet housecoat with a series of gold and diamond brooches depicting a mother bear and her three cubs. The second dining room, typically called the breakfast room owing to its multiple, high windows facing east, was bathed in morning sunlight. The moat rippled and glistened outside the windows and on its banks a chiffon of snow sparkled.

"I'm not a mind-reader, Glitz." Teddy was wearing a kimono and browsing the buffet, filtering and filching the least crispy kippers for Tuxedo Bird. "If you'd wanted me to nick that necklace and chuck it in the moat, you should have said so. I admit, it occurred to me, but you said that it was worth a bob or two."

"Oh, no, Teddy! You haven't thrown my necklace into the moat, have you?"

Teddy paused her probe for the perfect kipper and regarded her hostess.

"It's subtle, Glitz, but I'm clever about these things — has your necklace gone missing?"

"Sometime last night." Glitz sat heavily at the head of the table and stared blankly out at the grounds. "Oh, Teddy, I was so hoping that you'd done it."

"Wasn't it in the safe?"

"Yes, it was," said Glitz. "I thought you'd somehow managed to open it. I remember one summer at your parents' place in Berkshire you sneaked a toad into the vanity in our room."

"I climbed the water spout," said Teddy with the tone of one divulging the plainly obvious. "Child's play. Literally, in fact — I was nine."

"Oh, Teddy, whatever am I going to do?" Glitz held her head with both hands, as though to delay its departure. "When Tom finds out..."

"Topsy doesn't know?" Teddy introduced a cup into Glitz's line of vision and filled it with steaming calm.

"He knows the necklace was stolen." Glitz sipped her tea absently, forgetting that she took milk and two sugars. "He found the safe in his office open this morning. Empty." She put down her cup and looked at it, remembering that she took milk and two sugars.

"Then what are you concerned he might find out?"

"I cancelled the insurance policy."

"Oh, good," said Teddy. "Very timely. Why?"

"I just felt so utterly wretched when the thing was finally done, and it had cost so very, very..." Lady Gladys looked up and out at a distant, indifferent cloud, "...very much already."

"That's typically why we insure things, Glitz."

"Please don't ask me to explain my reasoning, Teddy." Glitz fortified her tea with three spoons of sugar. This was no time for milk. "I couldn't explain what I was thinking then and I'm even less able now. What's it called when you avoid something because you're afraid of jinxing it?"

"Thimble-witted?"

"I think I hoped it would be stolen," speculated Glitz, "and that if it was insured that was somehow less likely."

"Then yes, the word you're looking for is thimble-witted." Teddy took a bite of kipper which, out of respect for the extreme nature of the circumstances, she ate with her hands. "Are you going to call in the secular arm?"

"The police?" Ladies don't spit out their tea, but Glitz was sorely tempted. "The first they'll do is contact the insurance company."

"Why would they do that?"

"It's what they do in these cases, Teddy." Glitz added more refined white cope to her tea. "Ask Sir Oswald and Lady Dorothea. Nothing else was stolen from them but a necklace worth an absolute fortune — why investigate a robbery when it's an obvious case of insurance fraud."

"Well, it's probably for the best we don't involve the police," judged Teddy. "I'm not saying there is and I'm not saying there isn't, but it's not entirely impossible that there's a stolen penguin on the premises. So, what do we do?"

"We have to find it, Teddy." Glitz seized Teddy's eye in a fevered stare. "You have to find it."

"Very well." Teddy pointed at her with a kipper. "But if I'm to handle this affair, I must have a free hand. I shall need to question all witnesses, make all enquiries, and pursue the investigation no matter where it leads. And you, Lady Turville — you will have to be prepared to accept my conclusions, regardless of how distressing and disheartening they may be, and no matter which of your dearest friends may be implicated." Teddy took an earnest bite of kipper, to show that she meant what she said.

"Oh, no, Teddy," anguished Glitz. "No one can know there's been a robbery."

"Well, it stands to reason, Glitz, that someone already does."

"Teddy, you must find my necklace without letting anyone know you're looking for it."

"Fair enough," said Teddy. "Any other factors you think would be helpful? Would you like me to conduct the investigation from inside a locked steamer trunk?"

29

"It's ideal, Teddy." The hope rising in Lady Gladys was almost visible, indeed, her cheeks assumed a vague but rising hue of optimist pink. "Everyone will talk openly to you. All the boys want to know what you think, and everyone else wants to know what you think of the boys."

"Ah, now there you've identified a flaw in the plan, Glitz." Teddy raised a kipper and studied it for clues. "This approach you've outlined collides in a distinctly head-on manner with my rather concrete and pointy plan to encourage these three lambs to think twice about the institution of marriage and, in the case of Theodora Quillfeather, cease the practice of thinking about it altogether."

"Teddy — you promised your mother."

"I did nothing of the sort," objected Teddy judicially. "You promised my mother."

"Well, your mother promised me she'd take away your car and your flat."

"Yes, there is still that to be considered." Teddy bit off a meditative morsel of kipper. "Okay. I'll work out who took your hideous necklace and, if it turns out to be one of the boys, I'll marry him, and then send him off to prison. Everybody wins."

"That's the spirit." Glitz poured herself a happier cup of tea. She even added milk. "But you can't believe that any of our guests took it, surely."

"Who else?"

"When it happened at the Woolpit's place the police thought it must be a drifter."

"A drifter," said Teddy. "We're in a castle, Glitz, with an actual moat. And the safe was cracked. Drifting must be a far more exacting profession than it sounds."

"One of the staff?"

"No one is above suspicion," announced Teddy. "Do you know the combination to the safe, Glitz?"

"Me?"

"You."

"No, but why would I steal my own necklace?"

"Insurance fraud?"

"I've just told you — there isn't any insurance."

"Ah, yes, but you also confessed to being a thimble-wit," noted Teddy. "Maybe you forgot."

At that instant, the doors opened and Sir Oswald and Lady Dora blustered into the breakfast room. They, too, were country-house comfortable and, as do most members of the aristocracy when coming down to breakfast, they were wearing dressing gowns. Not all members of the aristocracy wear matching tartan dressing gowns with sky-blue satin cuffs, but it's not unheard of.

"Morning Teddy, Gladys," boomed Sir Oswald, and the couple made their way to the table via the sideboard.

"Good morning Oswald, Dora," replied Teddy and Glitz in some such variation, and Glitz added, "I was just telling Teddy about the burglary at the Hollows."

"Ah." Sir Oswald clattered to his place with a plate of kippers, soft-boiled eggs, and toasty soldiers. "Most extraordinary thing. Had the best minds of Scotland Yard utterly baffled."

"They said it must have been a drifter," added Dora.

"A drifter who knew the combination to the safe and that Dora's necklace would be in there which, under normal circumstances, it wouldn't have been," charged Oswald. "Drifter, forsooth."

"Did you tell me that the police suspected insurance fraud?" asked Glitz with all the offhand whimsy of a eulogy.

"They were certain of it," contended Oswald through a mouthful of eggy toast. "It's why they concocted this absurd drifter story. Why work an investigation when you're already sure who did it?"

"But the necklace was insured…" led Teddy.

"Yes, thanks to sheer chance," said Oswald.

"And Beau Pilewright," amended Dora. "He talked Oswald into taking out an insurance policy just two weeks before it happened."

"That's true." Oswald nodded at his egg. "Clever chap, that."

Lady Dora smiled meaningfully at Teddy and added, "And very wealthy."

"He mentioned," recalled Teddy. "Did he ever say anything to you about insanity in the family?"

"He most certainly did not." Dora's journalistic instincts were on alert and on display. "What did he say?"

"It just came up," said Teddy. "I'm not sure I can recall how."

"I'll just bet you it's his uncle Standish." Dora evinced a stage whisper like the steam brakes of a locomotive. "I hear that he had to be 'sent away' after he took all his savings and buried it, convinced that in due season he'd have an orchard of money trees."

"Yes, that must have been it." Teddy nodded sympathetically.

"And then he couldn't say where he planted it," continued Dora. "Somewhere in the city, was all he could remember."

"You won't say anything," presumed Teddy.

"My lips are sealed."

"You were saying, Sir Oswald," shifted Teddy, "that the necklace wouldn't normally have been in the safe. Why is that?"

Oswald had evacuated the egg and felled the soldiers, and was combing the remains from his moustache with a fork.

"For the same reason that the police couldn't work out who did it — we were all of us, including the staff, at the shoot."

"The Hollows is a shooting lodge," expanded Dora. "It would have been completely empty, so Mister Pilewright suggested that we lock up our valuables in the safe."

"Yes, you mentioned that he was there," recalled Teddy. "As was Algy Brookbridge."

"Terrible shot," commented Oswald. "Got one of the dogs in the hindquarters and himself in the foot."

"And Major Lonegrave was there," prompted Teddy.

"Excellent shot, you would have thought, but his gun jammed the first time, backfired the second, third time he stepped in a skunk's burrow," recounted Oswald. "Very nearly shot one of the beaters."

"When we got back to the lodge, the safe was open and my necklace was gone," summed up Dora with an awed, hushed emphasis on the word 'gone', as though finding a necklace missing was exactly as singular as finding a necklace talking.

"I suppose I ought to bring Tuxedo Bird his breakfast." Teddy stood and wrapped up the penguin's kippers. "He should be up by now — he went for a dip in the moat during the night. I hope he didn't disturb you."

"Was it around two o'clock?" asked Sir Oswald. "We did hear a bit of commotion around then."

"It was three o'clock," corrected Lady Dora. "But we soon went back to sleep."

"Ah, but you're in the west hall, first floor, above Lord Turville's study, aren't you," Teddy made a show of recalling. "Must have been something else."

"Probably a tycoon, or something," suggested Dora.

"We don't have tycoons in England, darling," gently corrected Oswald. "You're thinking of a macaroon."

"What ho, Topsy." Teddy popped her head through the door of Lord Turville's office.

"Oh, what ho, Teddy. You engaged yet?"

"Not yet." Teddy assumed the liberty of welcome and wandered deeper into the sanctum. "The short term forecast for hell is continued high temperatures and poor outlook for snowballs."

"Her Ladyship will be disappointed... oh, pox! I've recorded all that." Topsy took up a large speaking horn, the tube of which curled away to a complex composition of wires and wheels and widgets with a wax cylinder turning slowly in its centre. "Don't transcribe the bit starting from 'What ho' and ending with this bit right... now." He held up a shush hand. "Furthermore, the projected increased volume of phenol to one hundred and eight thousand gallons from one hundred and one thousand gallons can only be justified with a corresponding three point two percent decrease in the per gallon cost of methanal — with an 'a' — or a sustained power outage in south-east England... yours faithfully, etc."

Teddy, meanwhile, had been examining the combination safe on the bookshelf across from the door. It was, indeed, open and empty.

"This the unsafe safe?"

"Gladdy told you about it, did she?" Unlike everyone else but very much like Topsy, he was wearing a three-piece, pin-striped banking number with button-down collars and a school tie, the crest symmetrically centred between lapels, collar, and waistcoat. "She says she didn't want to accuse anyone before giving you right of first refusal."

"It wasn't me."

"I told her so," Topsy appeared to be dismantling his dictaphone. He removed the wax cylinder, then opened a panel in the wall revealing a lockbox, which he opened with a rapid combination. He locked up the cylinder and resumed his place behind his desk. "If you'd opened the safe it would have been to leave a toad, not take a necklace. Ah, Midgeham."

This last non sequitur was directed at the butler, who appeared at the door, triggering the reverse of the previous sequence.

"Take a cable, Midgeham…" Topsy gave the butler a moment to position cable book and pencil. "To the board of directors of Cheapside and Threadneedle Bank: 'No.' Take another cable to the chairman of the board of Cheapside and Threadneedle Bank: 'Yes.' Do not confuse them. And send this to my secretary in the City." He handed Midgeham the wax cylinder.

"Very good m'lord. Miss Giltspur asked me to mention, sir, that the quality of the recordings appears to be diminishing, and she is finding it increasingly difficult to transcribe your dictation."

"Rings like a clear, close bell on my machine."

"Miss Giltspur contends that your dictation machine is of an obsolete design, and recordings made on it are consequently only comprehensible when reproduced on the same machine."

"A new dictaphone costs twenty-nine pounds ten shillings six," reported Topsy. "I pay Miss Giltspur twenty two shillings nine a day. To justify the increased expenditure, a new machine would need to increase her productivity by eighteen percent over the course of six months, not accounting for holidays when I tend to write fewer letters, or nine hundred twenty nine words per day. In any case, I can't change machines. I need this one. I'll send her a dictaphone recording explaining it."

"Very good, m'lord." Midgeham shimmered away, closing the door behind him.

"Does Midgeham know the combination to the safe?" asked Teddy.

"Nobody knows the combination apart from me," claimed Topsy. "I change it every week. In any case, Teddy, if a member of the household staff meant to steal that necklace they'd obviously have done it prior to last night."

"Why not last night?"

"Because last night, exceptionally, it was in the safe," explained Topsy. "Usually it's in Gladdy's jewellery box on her dressing table. Easiest thing in the world to snatch it then."

"Why don't you normally keep it in the safe?" asked Teddy. "Or, put another way, why did you put it in the safe last night?"

"Consideration for the feelings of the Woolpits," said Topsy. "They had a burglary of their own. Now they're always going on about taking precautions. Frankly it was less painful just to put the thing in the safe than provide Oswald yet more cause to sermonise about the vital importance of vigilance."

"He's not really wrong, though, is he?" posited Teddy. "Glitz gave me to understand that it was worth a bomb."

"Seven thousand four hundred pounds, before tax," said Topsy. "Probably worth another thousand separated into its constituent parts. I paid seven thousand even just for the jade centrepiece."

"That monstrosity cost you seven thousand pounds," stounded Teddy. "That's twice what my flat cost, and I definitely overpaid. I really liked the colour."

"Monstrosity?"

"You can't go by me," retreated Teddy. "I don't care much for opera, either."

"Gladdy thinks one of our guests took it." Topsy withdrew his pipe in a worryingly knowing manner.

"She told me she was sure that they didn't," countered Teddy. "Who do you think she suspects?"

"No one, in particular." Topsy puffed his pipe up into an ominous cloud. "But she doesn't want me to call the police."

"She's asked me to try to work it out first," said Teddy. "I think she's just hoping to avoid scandal."

"Well, you'd best look slippy about it, Teddy. The police will have to be called in soon, if it's not recovered."

"Must they?"

"Of course," puffed Topsy. "Prerequisite to filing an insurance claim."

Tuxedo Bird, when Teddy returned to her room, had been for another dip in the moat and was now sleeping in her bed which was, to understate the case, damp. The penguin had taken with admirable aptitude to the pace and pitch of life in an English great house, for a flightless bird from the Antarctic. He'd been for a nice dip in the icy waters of the moat and, being a fully-grown adult male Emperor penguin, he'd eaten his six pounds of pike by six o'clock, and was now restoring his strength for what looked to be a trying afternoon shift.

So, when Teddy offered him a napkin-weight of kippers he deigned only open one eye, close it again, and turn away, seeking the cool spot on the pillow and pointing his beak, almost certainly unintentionally, to a little fold of paper on the nightstand.

This was the first Teddy had seen of the little fold of paper and so the dramatic effect was sorely muted, but it had been on the nightstand since four o'clock that morning, when Tuxedo Bird had seen the shadowy figure slip out the door.

The note, however, soon compensated for its inauspicious start with these three words, "Trust no one."

CHAPTER FOUR

In which Tilden rows a boat, Algy struggles to find something nice to say, and Beau doesn't.

"And what mischief did you get up to last night?"

Beauregard Pilewright, who had been lingering behind a planter column marking the north-west corner of the ground floor for ten minutes, made a very convincingly casual contrivance to accidentally encounter Teddy. Subtly reinforcing the impression of happenstance, he was wearing a cashmere Savile Row three-piece with the last button on his waistcoat undone, and he'd only shaved the one time.

"Oh, what ho, Bobo." Teddy's fight or flight or investigate jewel theft instincts fought a brief battle for control. "I was about to ask you the same thing."

"I waited for you in the drawing room for our walk in the garden."

"Did we say the drawing room for a walk in the garden?" asked Teddy. "I could have sworn we'd agreed the games room for a round of Chase the Dragon. They sound similar, don't they — drawing room, darts match."

"The wait only renders the reward that much sweeter," oozed Beau. "If you can spare me but a moment now, I would savour it for a year." He opened the door by which he'd been standing. "I can send for tea and... why, what good fortune — there appears to be a piano in this room."

Beau took a seat at the black baby grand and squinted at the sheet music. "I wonder if there's some little thing here to which my meagre talents are equal. *Ein Kleine Nachtmusik* by Mozart. Never heard of it, but it looks manageable enough." And instantly he was playing A Little Night Music as though he'd been practising it for years. "It's quite a nice little piece, this, isn't it?"

"I have a weakness for his earlier stuff. Do you know *Twinkle Twinkle?*" Teddy wandered across the ornate music room to the vast windows giving onto the Venetian scene of a balcony above the black waters of the moat.

"I hope my penguin didn't keep you up last night," directed Teddy. "His schedule's been all over the place since he quit coffee."

"I'm a man of calm and regular habits. I was in bed by ten and, after a few pages of an improving book, asleep by ten thirty."

"You didn't hear anything during the night?"

"I thought I heard your silvery laugh," sang Beau to the tune of Night Music. "But it turned out to only be a pleasant dream. Ah, Midgeham is here, and by happy coincidence it appears he's brought tea."

Midgeham had, by happy coincidence, brought tea. He laid out the tray and its trappings and discreetly withdrew. Teddy poured and prepared and reflected on the most subtle and effective approach to drawing out the suspect. When there's little physical evidence, a good detective will charm, disarm, and even befriend an interview subject. Finally, she struck just the right note.

"So, I understand your uncle is at the giggle-bin having his wig flipped round the right way."

"Dear old Uncle Standish." Beau sipped his tea with his right hand while his left danced Mozart's rhythm. "No, poor chap is in prison."

"Prison?"

"Shepton Mallet. Do you know it? Delightfully well-preserved example of a 17th century treadwheel house. Frightfully understaffed, at the moment — the inmates have to take turns guarding one another."

"Blimey." A student of body language, Teddy stood in the far corner. "No wonder you headline all that market maker and breaker snip."

"On the contrary — I'm most proud of Uncle Standish. He's an honest man serving an honest stretch at His Majesty's pleasure." Beau set down his cup and his right hand joined his left to really give Mozart his due. "Standish's only crime is sentiment, a commodity for which the City has no demand at all. He had among his clients — his oldest client, in fact — a wealthy woman of advanced age, who saw in her near future the beckoning of eternity. Her last and only desire was to see her son safely back in England — the boy was in Canada, you see, seeking his fortune, and had stumbled upon an unprecedentedly rich silver mine. She asked Standish to act as proxy and take all her money and buy the mine, freeing her son to return to England."

"And did he?"

"Alas, the poor old woman, comfortable as she was — her late husband happened to fall asleep while playing roulette in Monte Carlo, letting his accumulated stake ride on the night the pearl famously landed on black twenty-six times in a row — she couldn't afford the entire mine herself. Ah, this bit looks complicated..."

Beau met and mastered the Menuetto Allegretto.

"Oh, no, quite manageable..." he said. "So, Standish directed the funds of some of his other clients — with their full consent — into the purchase of the silver mine. Had it worked out, after all, they'd have been considerably wealthier for their trouble."

"There was no mine?" guessed Teddy.

"There was indeed a mine," differed Beau, with accompaniment by Beau. "And it was bountiful, but the lad, on seeing how easy it was to sell, proceeded to sell it three more times."

"Hardly the fault of Uncle Standish," pointed out Teddy.

"Your gentle mercy becomes you," flattered Beau. "My uncle's investors did not see it that way. They would have their pound of flesh, be it that of a sweet little old widow or prime Pilewright porterhouse."

"You're saying that your uncle went to prison on this woman's behalf?"

"With a song in his heart." Beauregard's eyes twinkled and the ivories tinkled. "He is a fool for the charms of humanity's finer half — a family trait shared by all Pilewright men."

Beau wound up the Finale Allegro and turned his attention to tea while his left hand considered another go. "Honesty, too, is a family trait."

"Oh, mine too," alleged Teddy. "Essentially a Quillfeather byword."

"Then I look forward to a meeting of minds with your father," lyricised Beau. "I have many profitable investments to put to him." *Ein Kleine Nachtmusik* began again. "Did you know, for instance, that Lord Turville is on the cusp of revolutionising the domestic adhesives market?"

"He's developed a secret formula called Stickle," furnished Teddy.

"What an extraordinary woman you are," serenaded Beau.

"Oof, that's nothing," waved away Teddy. "Adhesives and light industrials are just about all we talk about at the auto club. Why don't you put it to Algy Brookbridge or Stilts Stollery? Such gold as fill their pockets they'd both sink to the bottom of a vat of cold molasses."

"I daresay they would," agreed Beau, "but Algernon Brookbridge's father is Brookbridge Industrial Adhesives, who have products in direct competition to Stickle, and Tilden Stollery's family are exclusively in the precious gems trade." Beau paused the rhythm briefly to add, "I tried."

"The Woolpits, then," suggested Teddy. "Or do they already think too highly of you already?"

"Sir Oswald and Lady Woolpit enjoy a lavish income which almost precisely matches their lavish outgoing," said Beau. "They would have difficulty affording gratuities were it not for Sir Oswald's absent-mindedness — he always seems to be forgetting his wallet at home."

"Is that why you advised them to insure Lady Dora's necklace?"

"That is precisely why," replied Beau. "They are among the privileged cash-poor, and a shock to their finances would be ruinous. If you're failing to keep track, Teddy, you can so far credit my campaign with wealth, wisdom, calm and regular habits, scruples, and a warm and abiding concern for my fellow man."

"Got it."

"I'll send you a short summary."

"That would be very helpful." Teddy topped up their tea. "And you were on hand when the Woolpit necklace was, indeed, stolen."

"I was." Beau wound up the second *Kleine* of *Nachtmusik* and took up his cup. "A most baffling set of circumstances."

"Everyone was murdering grouse, at the time, I understand," understood Teddy.

"Pheasant," corrected Beau. "All within sight of one another."

"And so the police concluded that it was a drifter."

"So I understand," said Beau. "Drifters, they would have us believe, are at any given time roaming the countryside in their thousands, passing through locked doors and popping open safes with some sort of advanced drifter technology."

"You don't believe it?"

"Of course not," scoffed Beau. "Lady Dora's necklace must have been stolen by someone who was present at the hunt."

❦

"It was a drifter."

Algernon Brookbridge issued this bold challenge to received wisdom from the safety of the garden island of Hardy Holm. Snow had fallen heavily during the night and now, in the early afternoon, the sunny skies of Kent looked down on bare trees and bushes and beech bowers piped with white icing, and a crisp silvery frost of lawn. Algy and Teddy paused their walk to watch Tuxedo Bird toboggan past, take flight briefly against a rise in the bank of the moat over which he briefly hovered before plopping into the water with nary a splash.

"Why do you say that?" Teddy had added a fur shawl and ankle boots to her ensemble, as is advised when walking one's penguin. Algy was in a black woollen overcoat which had been left behind by a previous guest at Hardy Hall who, by all appearances, had no shoulders.

"Well, I mean to say, wasn't it?" puzzled Algy. "It's what the police said."

"You can't always go by what the police say," warned Teddy. "Only last month a constable stood up in Bow Street Magistrates' and swore — under oath — that I'd abandoned my car in the garden at Leicester Square."

"Oh, right. Yes, I see…"

"It was parked," clarified Teddy. "Abandoned indeed — I was late for an appointment with a jockey of my acquaintance who had very perishable information to relay. Am I expected to drive around all day looking for a place to park?"

"It's just difficult to imagine who else might have done it," said Algy. "We were all at the hunt."

"Where you shot yourself in the foot, I understand."

"Just a bit." Algy held up his right foot and cocked his head at it. "I felt much worse about the dog. He didn't seem so much injured as disappointed in me, if you take my meaning."

"He trusted you."

"Not once I'd shot him, he didn't." Algy gazed off into a painful past. "My father often looks at me like that."

"Brookbridge Industrial Adhesives," reminded Teddy.

"That's the chap."

"I suppose he does business with Lord Turville."

"No." The word appeared to pain Algy, so he took another run at it. "I mean to say, yes." This, too, failed to give complete satisfaction. "It's a bit murky. They were working together on something that I'm not meant to be talking about, you see…"

"Stickle."

"That's the stuff," spotted Algy. "Or, rather, no. Not that."

"There must be no secrets between us, Algy, if you're going to keep your promise to your mother."

"Oh, right oh." Algy reflected on this dilemma, aided in reaching a decision by the categorical omen of a penguin porpoising the length of the moat. "Yes, my father and Lord Turville developed Stickle together, but there's since been a sort of falling out over how it's brought to market — my father wanted it to be an exclusive product of Brookbridge Industrial Adhesives, and Lord Turville wanted to licence the patent."

"And yet, here you are," observed Teddy.

"That's all just business, isn't it?" Algy watched Tuxedo Bird do another pass. "And Lady Turville is quite friendly with my mother."

"Talking of which…" Teddy, seizing the sign, introduced the subtext of criminal psychology, "…days are short this side of the solstice. You'll want to present your case while you can. You should know, in all fairness, that you're up against a piano-playing portfolio of calm and regular habits."

"I don't really know where to start…"

"Bobo sent me a handy chart, would you like to refer to it for inspiration?" offered Teddy. "It's colour-coded."

"No, that's all right." Seeking distraction, Algy shook the spindly birch under which he stood, causing it to pot him with a branchload of snow. "Let's see, I got my Oxford Blue for rugby, but wasn't much of a student. I switched my course of study a few times..."

"Loads of my friends did that, too."

"I say a few times..." Algy contorted like a man as a claw of snow slid down his neck. "Twelve."

"Are there twelve courses of study at Oxford?" asked Teddy.

"Six of them were chemistry," explained Algy. "My father was quite insistent. After the fire, though..."

"What fire?"

"Well, the last one. The first four weren't regarded as sufficiently serious to warrant kicking me out."

"I see. Carry on."

"Let's see..." Algy drew an asymmetric circle in the snow with his foot. "I'm not very musical, I'm a rather famously poor public speaker, my aptitude for firearms I think you already know..."

"I mean your good qualities, Algy," suggested Teddy, helpfully. "You know, why I should consider your candidacy for the role of my first husband."

"Oh, right, yes, I see what you mean." Algy traced the circle the other direction. "I scored three tries in the Oxford-Cambridge Varsity Match in my final year, I have excellent eyesight, and I can lift the back end of an Austin Seven."

"There you go," lauded Teddy. "All those talents and triumphs obscured by a couple of small fires and literally shooting yourself in the foot. I'll bet you're a man of very refined tastes, too."

"You're not going to ask me about art, are you?" Algy led on as they continued the circuit around the moat. "I once wrote a paper about Monet for an art history elective, except I confused him with that other chap..."

"Manet."

"Michelangelo," admitted Algy. "They keep the paper on display at Merton College Library."

"Taste isn't just about knowing your impressionists from your renaissance men," said Teddy. "What do you make of Hardy Hall?"

"It's very nice." Algy stood and took in the grounds, hands on hips. "This would make an excellent rugby pitch, without all these trees."

"Very well, then... what about Lady Turville's necklace?"

"What necklace?"

"You didn't notice her necklace?" doubted Teddy.

"That mouldy green and gold thing that looked like it grew out of some damp?" asked Algy.

"You recall it, then."

"Let's see — seven rows of four, three, nine, one, three, seven, and five jadestones above a goose egg of an emerald." Algy spoke as though describing squirrel pie. "Yes, I recall it."

"You didn't think much of it, then?"

"Did you?"

"It's meant to be worth a fortune."

"So's Kent Coal Field," posited Algy. "Wouldn't want to wear it round my neck."

Algy and Teddy had done roughly half a turn around the castle which, counting the moat, was a similar distance to half a turn around Croydon Racecourse. Tuxedo Bird, however, had gone around six times, including once on his stomach across the snow. Fatigued, he now hopped up onto a first-floor balcony where Portion was waiting — and had been for twenty minutes — with a tin of sardines.

"What ho, Ports," hailed Teddy. Portion looked up and, because she was wearing her glasses, smiled in warm recognition, and waved. Then she removed her glasses and hid them in a vase.

"Have you met Portia Beanfield?" Teddy asked Algy. "Lovely girl. Lovely person. You want someone who knows and appreciates the value of brute strength and good eyesight in a chap, there's your girl."

"No," wavered Algy, noncommittally, as though unsure from that distance if Portion wasn't a garden gnome. "I mean to say, we were introduced when I arrived, of course."

Tuxedo Bird, apparently sardine-drunk, waddled to the edge of the balcony and dropped into the water like a felled tree.

"Oh, I say, I hope that my penguin and I didn't keep you up last night," spurred Teddy. "We argued over a fillet of mackerel, one thing led to another, and, as you've probably guessed, we settled it with a swimming race." Teddy mirrored Algy's vacant smile. "He won. I probably should have known better."

"In fact, I did hear you last night." Algy nodded vacantly. "Saw you, too, I think. I was coming from the library."

"You sure it was me?"

"It was dark," acknowledged Algy. "But it was definitely a woman. Quite a bit shorter than you, now I think of it. She came out of your room and walked right into the planter column."

🍂

"I didn't hear a thing last night. The champagne cocktails hit me like a hammer, as it were." Tilden Stollery broke this bold, bumpkin admission and quickly added, "Oh, sorry, Tedds," because he then slipped an oar, dishing Teddy a course of pond water, again.

"Quite all right, Stilts." Teddy shook off a shiver of river. "It's refreshing. Like being slapped awake with a salmon."

47

They were in a punt, as promised, in the early twilight of post-teatime Kent in the winter, on the slow and sloppy pond surrounding Hardy Holm. The waters of Pool Hardy are meant to be refreshed on a roughly quarterly basis by the river Newel which is also the sole means of support for two irrigation canals and a reservoir and so, understandably, it often neglects its duties to the little pond altogether. The water is consequently still and smells just a little bit like corked wine, but it's tremendously well-suited to the improvisational oarsmanship of Stilts Stollery. The pond is also a reflective surface of weeping willows and lilypads, bulrushes and sedge grass, and cosy coves and dozy groves. In short, all the ageless serenity and amenity that Stilts would need, had he a single ounce more poetry in his soul, to stage a positive pastoral of a proposal.

Stilts, however, was wearing a deerstalker hat. He'd further nobbled himself right out of the gate with an Inverness Cape and wellies. Finally and fully stymying his chances — very much gilding the lily — was the fact that he was Stilts Stollery in charge of a rowboat.

"Sorry." Stilts slipped both oars this time for such a well-targeted double he might have been aiming at Teddy's head.

"Do you want me to row?"

"I think I'm getting a grip on it, now." He lost an oar. "Oh."

Teddy recovered the oar as it floated past but held it in trust. "Let's just float a bit, Stilts."

"Oh, right, yes, excellent." Stilts put up the other oar and assumed an awkwardly deliberate insouciance. He regarded the bank with a noble bearing. "Lovely spot, this. Makes me think of that rather natty saw by Shelley... How does it go again... Oh, yes, I recall."

He cleared his throat.

"I wondered lonely among the crowds..."

"I wandered lonely as a cloud," corrected Teddy. "Wordsworth."

"Quite right." Stilts, to his credit, reversed and took another run.

"I wandered lonely as a cloud,
Way up there over yonder hills,
When all at once I saw a crowd — oh, right, that's when the crowd bit comes in…
A host of golden daffodils,
Beside the lake and beneath the trees,
Prancing and flancing about my knees, as it were."

"Very much in the spirit of the original," encouraged Teddy. "Go on."

"That's it."

"Three more verses, I think you'll find."

"Blimey. Is it an epic?" gogged Stilts. "That's all I memorised. I know the lyrics to *Yes, We Have No Bananas.* Most of them, at least."

"Save it for dinner, in case conversation wains," advised Teddy. "Did you know the Woolpits before coming down to Hardy Hall?"

"Only by name." The boat drifted into some willow branches, taking Stilts by surprise, but he gamely fought them off. "Tell you who's a dire bit of leg-before-wicket, though, is that Beauregard Pilewright."

"So, you've never been to the Woolpit's hunting lodge, The Hollows."

"No, never." Stilts discreetly spat out a willow leaf. "Talking of hollow, have you spent more than two minutes with that Brookbridge object? You stand close enough you can hear the echo. Stand far enough away and he forgets you were ever there."

"He seemed quite nice." Teddy used her oar to push away from where the little punt had run aground on a deceptive underwater atoll.

"Quite nice." Stilts tried to paddle but got his oar stuck in the lakebed. "Mama has a Yorkie who'll happily spend an entire day barking at a reproduction of Landseer's *Stag at Bay."* His oar was stuck. "He's quite nice, though."

"I found his modesty rather charming."

"Modesty?" bridled Stilts. "Going on about his rugby blue and double first at Oxford? If that's modesty to you, Theodora Quillfeather, then let me provide you an exhaustive list of every single comportment ribbon I received throughout a frankly unblemished career at prep."

"Algy has a double first from Oxford?" puzzled Teddy. "I thought he changed course six times."

"So he did. Ended up in English and Classics. Cheated his way to a double first."

"Really?" Teddy proffered the oar. "Can you be trusted with this? No fibbing, Stilts — I'll know."

"I can do only my best."

"Algy cheated a double first out of Oxford?" Teddy returned to a favoured theme.

"Well, no, or rather, yes." Stilts fitted the oar back into the oarlock. "Not the clever, rebellious sort of evasion that you like. He memorised a stack of poetry and the Iliad and whatnot. If that's not cheating then I suppose there's no such thing."

"Well, that's just lazy."

"Exactly my point."

"You'll want to turn us around, now, Stilts," skippered Teddy. "Just operate the oars in opposite directions."

In point of fact, operating the oars in opposite directions had been more-or-less what Stilts had been doing from the outset, and yet now that he was asked to do so the instinct completely failed him.

"And what do you make of Bobo Pilewright?" asked Teddy to pass the time while waiting for Stilts to acquire adult motor skills.

"Oh, delightful chap." Stilts, endeavouring to pull in opposite directions, was finally making way in one direction. "Provided you have a taste and tolerance for blustering great egos with a pig in a poke for every occasion. He tried to sell me shares, in chronological order, in his own brokerage, a new footbridge over the Thames serving the thriving new residential community of Thamesmead, the new residential community of Thamesmead, beer, corn futures, and, when I told him politely but firmly that my interests are limited to precious stones, my own family's diamond mine."

"Not a good bet?"

"The mine is doing swimmingly." Stilts managed a certain cool disdain while struggling with the oars. "It requires no external investment."

"Which brings us back to the Woolpit question," redirected Teddy. "Did you know that Lady Woolpit's necklace was stolen during a shooting weekend attended by just about everybody who's here this weekend?"

"Oh, yes." In that same instant, Stilts found the rhythm of opposing oars and the boat began to turn back towards home. "Nothing of that magnitude happens in the jewellery business without the family firm catching wind of it, as it were."

"Talking of which, Stilters, did you happen to notice the necklace that Lady Turville was wearing before dinner last night?" casually commented Teddy, while dangling a disinterested finger in the water.

"Rather hard to miss." Stilts gave a spirited pull on the oars and the boat went into a continuous spin. "Hideous great thing. It's regarded as something of a notorious tragedy in Bond Street circles. There was talk of a royal enquiry."

"Surely it's not that bad."

"Surely it is, Tedds," Stilts assured her. "In any case, the tragedy to which I refer is the dark deed visited upon the original, uncut emerald — it was a flawless example of the type; uniform aquamarine, luminous, limpid clarity, a hypnotically flawless and complex crystal structure that you want to swim in and somehow has about it a light perfume of lime custard. And Lady Turville imprisoned it in that gaudy gilded gasworks. I swear I could almost hear it crying out for help last night."

"And how did Lady Turville, whose taste in jewellery, between you and me, compares unfavourably to a particularly extroverted Christmas tree, warrant such a prize stone?"

"Ah, well, they're personal friends with the chap who brought it back from Burma, aren't they? Story goes that the chap was anxious to be rid of it." Stilts dug the oars into the water, set and synchronised, and heaved a solid, satisfying cull that drove the boat directly into the bank. "You know him as well, in point of fact — Major Lonegrave."

CHAPTER FIVE

Which explores the universal metaphor that is snooker, reveals the wardrobe secrets of the modern flapper, and follows the beak of suspicion, wherever it points.

"What ho, Tedds." Portion was positioned on a pile of pillows, wrapped in a blanket and wearing specs like jeweller's loupes. She had taken the liberty of the floor of Teddy's room, availing of the licence automatically reciprocated among single ladies staying at country houses. The pillows, fried smidgen shrimp, and penguin were, perhaps, exceptional, but well short of out-of-bounds. "Watch this."

Tuxedo Bird was nested on a plump pasha pillow of his own and in the moment he was dodging his head from side-to-side like a goalkeeper. Portion selected a smidgen shrimp from a glass porringer on the floor next to her, took careful aim, and darted it just above the bird's head. Tuxedo Bird watched it sail above him and continued to follow the trajectory until he tipped over backwards.

"That's twelve in a row," counted Portion. "He's a delightful bird, Tedds, but your penguin is as dim as a doused candle."

"I know it." Teddy traded her wrap for a plush dressing gown. "On the way down from London he was in charge of the map. We nearly wound up in Sussex." She opened and surveyed the drinks cabinet. "'Go south' — it's his answer to everything."

"Did you fall in love by the moat?" asked Portion.

"I fell in love *with* the moat." Teddy improvised something approaching a shaker of Gin Gimlets. "How can the Turvilles afford their own island on an island?"

"They can't...Oh! Good catch, Tux... Topsy put it on the cuff, apparently in anticipation of a whacking great payout on some tremendous innovation — a perpetual motion machine or powdered whisky or something of that nature."

"It's glue, apparently, and the smart money is betting that it's going to pay off very handsomely." Teddy paused to give the cocktails a shaking they'd remember. "So long as he's able to keep it secret until kickoff."

"So you didn't instantly fall under the spell of three tries at the Varsity Match and a verbatim recitation of every single poem from Wordsworth to Coleridge?" Portion accepted a fizzy coupe of gimlet. "Cheers."

"Algy steered clear of the Romantics," recounted Teddy. "Not sure why. Probably wanted to make sure there was time to mention that he could lift the back end of a Morris Seven."

"Austin Seven." Portion arced another shrimp over Tuxedo Bird's head. "How about contestant number two?"

"Bobo?" Teddy sat on the bed to watch the age-old contest of penguin versus flapper. "I really don't think I could compete — no one will ever love Beauregard Pilewright the way Beauregard Pilewright does."

"He's rich, handsome, clever, musical — have you heard him play *Eine Kleine Nachtmusik?* — and he's charming," inventoried Portion. "And your complaint is that he's got elevated self-esteem." She lobbed Tuxedo Bird an easy one. It bounced off his head. "I take it then that you're going to accept Stilts Stollery. He's got the ego of a clumsy penguin."

"There is that," acknowledged Teddy. "But they all three lack the one thing I need in a husband."

"What more could you possibly want?"

"Age, Portion." Teddy sipped her gimlet reflectively. "They're none of them old enough."

"They're all three your age, almost exactly."

"Precisely — I'm not old enough either. I need, say, another ten years, or until my liver gives out, whichever comes second."

"Didn't you very nearly marry Pimms Holloway?" Portion spun Tuxedo Bird another googly which he neatly plucked out of the air and celebrated with a turn around the pillow, flapping his wings.

"Dear Pimms," reminisced Teddy. "The love of my life. The love of last end-of-summer, certainly. He wanted to marry me on his yacht. Were it not for two simple fatal flaws, who knows what might have been."

"What flaws? Or, rather, what flaws could he have had that you don't have in sacks?"

"First, it turned out he was serious," recounted Teddy. "Worst, my mother liked him, the poor nit. Not his fault, really, but what are you going to do?"

"How did you break it off?"

"In point of fact, I didn't — he did. I mean to say, his mother did, but it was poor Pimms who had to deliver the blow — it seems his mother got hold of one of those anti-monarchist tracts with my father's byline."

"Your father wrote an antimonarchist tract?" marvelled Portion. "I thought he was just marginally more establishment than King George."

"I expect that's why Mater Holloway was so shocked and disappointed," reasoned Teddy. "I probably could have just printed up a criticism of a return to the gold standard or support for the beer tax, but I didn't want to drag things out — regatta season was just about to kick off."

"Is that your plan for this lot?"

"Regrettably not." Teddy drew thoughtfully on her cocktail. "This weekend's candidates have been fully sounded and certified by Mama, as part of a larger conspiracy. There's no telling how high this thing goes. No, this will require three unrelated, unconventional, custom conceived and coldly and boldly executed countermeasures. Apropos of nothing at all, have you any dynamite?"

Portion moved a shrimp in a slow, hypnotic circle. Tuxedo Bird followed the movement like a predator, and then tired of the game and communicated as much with a hop and flap that were difficult to misinterpret. Portion tossed him the shrimp, which he missed.

"Algy, I can understand, he's a big dumb rock who, you just can tell by looking, is bound to break some valued family heirloom," observed Portion with clinical objectivity. "But Beauregard is the kind of bloke who winds up getting invited to the palace where he's accidentally knighted, and Stilts yearns but for a petal from a rose that knows another rose that you once wore in your hair."

"Yes, but can any of them be trusted?" wondered Teddy.

"Why shouldn't they?" wondered Portion right back, which was dashed good timing and fortune from Teddy's perspective, because until that moment she believed that it had been Portion who had left a note in her room warning that no one could be trusted. Teddy had been about to divulge the truth about the current disposition of Lady Turville's necklace.

"No reason," idled Teddy. "Did you know that Algy and Bobo were at Sir Oswald and Lady Woolpit's hunting lodge the weekend that her necklace was stolen?"

"You don't think one of them is a jewel thief," derided Portion. "They were both at the shoot, like everyone else."

"Just a tick — you were at The Hollows the weekend that Lady Dora's necklace was stolen from the Woolpit's safe?"

"Of course." Portion showed Tuxedo Bird a particularly plump shrimp and then ate it herself.

Beyond the French doors the winter evening was now a satin black. Teddy gazed at the glass which reflected the scene in the room, and she knew that she could, indeed, trust no one.

❦

Major Stanley Lonegrave was in the games room, playing snooker against himself and, somehow, losing.

"Evening Major." Teddy wandered idly into the room while simultaneously thinking of a pretext for doing so. "I was wondering if they had a bagatelle table."

"Do you play bagatelle?"

"Never!" aspersed Teddy. "That's why I wanted to make sure there wasn't a table on the premises. One can never be too careful."

"No indeed." The major bent to line up an easy straightaway from cue ball to red, he slid the stick lightly and tightly, missed the red altogether, and sank the black. "Ah."

"Shall I officiate, Major?" asked Teddy, recovering and replacing the black. She'd dressed for dinner in a warm woollen evergreen ball gown and wrap, but this was an informal match.

The major had also already changed for dinner and was now wearing his evening safari jacket, along with jodhpurs and laced jungle boots. His bamboo whangee hung on the cue rack.

"You'll want to stand clear," warned the major. "My snooker game is most remarked upon for its casualties. Once took the eye out of an officiator in Jaipur. Disqualified, of course. And the chap was the son of a local sultan. There's still a price on my head in Rajputana."

Major Lonegrave lined up the exact same shot again, executed it in exactly the same manner, and this time sank the pink.

"Hard luck, Major." Teddy recovered and replaced the ball and marked '-6' on the scoreboard. "Have you spent a great deal of time in the east?"

"East, west, antipodes…" The major executed an almost impossible ricochet to snooker himself between the green, the pink, the yellow, and a corner pocket. "And Tahiti, but I didn't go there willingly."

"You were kidnapped?"

"Shipwrecked." Lonegrave reset the cue ball. "You're thinking of Vanuatu. Lovely coastline, going by what I could see from the prison hulk."

"How did you escape?" goggled Teddy.

"Well, I didn't, in fact. They tried to ransom me but the first messengers sank in a freak storm and the second were blown off course to Japan, of all places, where they decided to settle," the major narrated as Teddy reracked the balls. "The third were themselves kidnapped and before they could send another delegation, a monsoon flooded their village. In the end they gave me a boat and a bottle of rum and shot at me until I was over the horizon."

"What extraordinary luck you've had, Major."

"Oh, don't be deceived by all that, young lady," advised Lonegrave. "Much of my luck has been quite bad."

"I understand that during your travels you became acquainted with Lady Gladys' necklace." Teddy stood a safe distance while the major lined up to break.

"Oh, yes, I know it intimately." Lonegrave pistoned the cue ball directly into the south-west pocket. "I stole it."

"Oh. Right. Well," fumbled Teddy. "That settles that, then. Are you going to give it back?"

"Give it back?" Scorned the major. "Why would I do that?"

"Because it's not yours?"

"No, I sold it to Lady Gladys," said Lonegrave, distractedly, as he took the shot again, this time popping the cue ball into a terra cotta vase. "Some good time after I stole it in Burma."

"Burma."

"Rangoon, to be precise, in 1919." Lonegrave leaned on his cue stick to reflect. "Just the centre stone, you understand. It was known then as The Spirit of Myawaddy. Beautiful gemstone. Flawless."

"From whom did you steal it?"

"River pirates operating along the Bago." Lonegrave replaced the cue ball and again fired it straight into the south-west pocket. "They had a very effective tactic of painting their boats to look like border patrols and ostensibly searching barges for contraband and, of course, impounding whatever took their fancy. Easily done, because nobody knows what border patrol boats look like. One day they happened upon a bunch of missionaries who were trying to smuggle The Spirit of Myawaddy out of Burma."

"Missionaries?"

"Not real missionaries, no." Lonegrave finally made a clean break, sinking nothing. "Australian raiders, disguised as monks. They had appropriated The Spirit of Myawaddy from a band of Moroccan thieves who were travelling South-East Asia, passing themselves off as an ensemble ballet company. No idea who they stole it from, but the chain eventually leads back to a little mine somewhere near the border of Siam."

"And how did you get it?"

"Nothing very clever, I'm afraid." Lonegrave made his first clean shot, sinking a red which popped right back out of the pocket and rolled back to where it started. "Got to talking to them in a bar in Rangoon — we were playing Pitch Penny using the emerald instead of a penny, and they were telling me about this tremendous run of poor luck they'd been having. Seems just about every boat they'd stopped on the river turned out to be real border patrol, the boats of which, apparently, have no markings at all. All they had left was The Spirit of Myawaddy."

"And yet you were able to get it away from them?" doubted Teddy.

"In fact, they left it in my care while they all went to visit a sick friend."

"Some river pirates left a priceless gem with you while they went to visit a sick friend?"

"Well, just so…" The major reproduced the previous shot, but this time the red banked, twice, sinking the black and the yellow. "Didn't strike me as odd, at the time, so I just put it in my pocket, walked out of the bar, and stowed away aboard a banana boat bound for home. On reflection I realise that they were trying to get rid of the thing."

"Why was that, do you suppose?" Teddy changed the score to -15.

"The banana boat ran aground off Andaman. The river pirates had never seen a border patrol before they got ahold of The Spirit of Myawaddy, and then that's all they saw. The Australian raiders were arrested, to a man, and deported to New Zealand. The Moroccan thieves lost their lead dancer to a rival gang of gunrunners and their choreographer left over creative differences. In short, The Spirit of Myawaddy is bad juju." In quick succession and without first sinking a red, the major pocketed the brown, pink, black, and yellow.

"Then — and I hope you'll take this in the spirit in which it's intended, Major…" Teddy chalked the score down to -34, "…why in the blue devil did you sell it to friends?"

"Why, for the money." The major, finally, put up his cue. "That's the point, you see, the ill fortune only attends those who steal The Spirit of Myawaddy."

"And so you sold it to Lord and Lady Turville for a fair price, one can assume," assumed Teddy.

"In fact, no, I believe that they grossly overpaid, considering the dubious origins of the gem," said the major with a flat, innocently academic detachment.

"Did overcharging them somehow diminish the effects of the curse?"

"Now you come to say it, that may just be so." The major retrieved his whangee for the purpose of whacking it thoughtfully against his leg, in the manner of the imperial plantation bwana. "But

I didn't set the price — in fact I was paid a paltry sum for the jewel. Just glad to be rid of it."

"Well, then, who brokered the sale?"

"Chap named Stitch Stollery. In fact, he's the father of that tall chap who moons about you all the time — Tilts, is it?"

"Stilts," said Teddy, distractedly.

❦

Tuxedo Bird was on the balcony, looking in, and looking disappointed.

Teddy is quick-witted. She's one of those swift stilettas who navigate after-hours London without ever paying for a drink or giving her real name to a police constable. She knew that she'd left the French doors open so Tuxedo Bird could enjoy the night air and Lord Turville's stock of moat pike from the convenience of home. She knew that because these same doors were now closed, someone must have been in her room. She had other things on her mind, though, and hadn't yet worked out that this person was still there.

Tuxedo Bird hopped and flapped in that helpless yet insistent way common to his kind, and Teddy opened the door and let him in. He waddled, wings fully deployed, across the room to the wardrobe at which he hissed like a kettle that's tired of being ignored. Finally, Teddy connected these clues into a stark realisation.

"I know you're in there," she announced, putting on a brave face made almost entirely of gin. "You should know that I'm terrified, and that I have a scream in me that could shatter a diamond."

After a brief period of reflection, the wardrobe door creaked slowly open to reveal a later middle-aged woman of thin and recessive posture, wearing a floor-length terry-weave dressing gown and wool scarf and hiding behind a trench coat.

"Aunty Azalea?" Teddy asked with surprised surmise.

"Oh, hello Teddy," squeaked Azalea Boisjoly, Teddy's aunt by marriage. "How nice to see you."

"You should catch me when I'm not scared half out of my skin," advised Teddy. "What are you doing in my wardrobe?"

"I heard someone coming." Azalea spoke in hushed, harried tones.

"Just now you mean? That was me."

"Well, yes." Azalea, after a quick glance around the room, stepped out of the wardrobe. "I know that now."

Azalea, as has been mentioned, is hidebound. She's timid, in much the same way and to much the same degree that penguins are flightless. Her most intimate and active social commerce is with her milkman, with whom she communicates strictly by typewritten note.

"Did Glitz not provide you with your own wardrobe to hide in?" asked Teddy.

"I wanted to see you." Aunty Azalea turned the key in the door.

"You couldn't have just made an appointment with my secretary, like everyone else? My hours of operation are very flexible, and walk-in consultations can often be accommodated."

"We must speak most discreetly, Teddy." Azalea closed the French doors while Tuxedo Bird followed her with a suspicious eye.

"What does that mean by your standards, Aunts?" Teddy wondered. "Must we first develop a secret language known only to ourselves? Invisible ink that no one, not even we, can read?"

"Your mother sent me." Aunty Azalea, though she knows Teddy well, seemed to think that carried weight.

"I know." Teddy limbered up her fingers before the drinks cabinet. "Glib gimlet?"

"Please. Your mother wants to make sure that you behave while at Hardy Hall."

"Behave." Teddy rolled the word over on her tongue, as though wondering if she was pronouncing this alien idiom correctly. "Why wouldn't I?"

"I expect your mother was thinking of the occasion of your visit to Kingsclere Castle."

"How is any of that my fault?" Teddy shook the cocktail shaker, in deference to Azalea's sensibilities, violently. "Basil Pewsey should never have said he could handle a runaway horse unless he expected to have the claim tested."

"Or the regrettable occurrence at the Hudson-Birch country house."

"That was a special commission, done on behalf of a very dear cousin who had cause." Teddy handed over a fizzy gimlet. "Anyway, they were temporary tattoos."

"Spencer Hudson-Birch didn't know that, though, did he."

"No he most certainly did not." Teddy toasted and drank to the fond memory. "What's gotten into mother, anyway? Why is this weekend so special?"

"It's your mother's view that you're not getting any younger."

"She's always been good with numbers, Mama."

"I gather that's what's at issue." Azalea peered wide-eyed over the top of her gimlet. "Your father's invested a tremendous amount of money in some secret project of Lord Turville's — Stickso or Stick Man or something."

"Stickle," provided Teddy.

"Stickle." Azalea looked quickly from side-to-side before briefly giggling. "Apparently they're at some very delicate point in bringing it to market and your mother says if it doesn't go well she'll have to sell your flat in Chelsea."

"This again."

"And the house in Berkshire."

"Ah. That's new." Teddy swirled a meditative gimlet. "I understand that it's all in hand, though, so long as the secret formula remains a secret. And you can tell Mama that I'm being the perfect houseguest — you know, of course, that Glitz's necklace has gone missing."

"Did you take it, dear?"

"No, I didn't take it," scoffed Teddy. "For one thing, it's hideous. I am discreetly working out who did take it, though. Did you not know that there'd been a burglary?"

"No."

"Then was it not you who left me a note saying 'trust no one'?"

"Oh, yes, that was me." Azalea nodded at her gimlet. "I just think it's good advice."

"Particularly now," agreed Teddy. "I've got a house full of suspects."

"Your mother also said that you're to be your nicest possible self to the boys that she's arranged to be here this weekend."

"That vexing woman — how am I to conduct an investigation if I can't beat suspects with rubber hoses and refuse to marry them?"

"You don't think any of them stole Lady Gladys' necklace," ghasted Azalea.

"They've got motive, just like everyone else," Teddy professed professoraly. "Which is to say, not at all. Not really, anyway. Bobo — Beauregard Pilewright — might have done it just because there's something rather dashing about jewel thieves."

"Is there?"

"Well, obviously," said Teddy. "Like pirates and men who play the saxophone. As for Algy — Algernon Brookbridge — his family is rich as plum pudding and he's about as dashing as, well, also plumb pudding. Then there's Tilden Stollery — Stilts to you and me and anyone who's seen him, even from a great distance — who might have taken it with a mind to putting it out of its misery."

"You mustn't accuse any of them of theft," warned Azalea. "Your mother would never invite me back to Chipping Chase."

"You never go anyway."

"I like to be asked." A tick of a clock or click of a lock pricked Azalea's cat-like reflexive fear of making small talk with strangers. "What was that?"

"Oh, that'll just be Midgeham, loading his six-shooter. It's how dinner's announced at Hardy Hall." Teddy finished her gimlet. "Still plenty of time to inventory the suspects. Next is probably Sir Oswald and Lady Dorothea Woolpit — they're the only possibilities with anything like a motive. According to Bobo they're quite cash poor, in spite of an insurance settlement on a jewel heist of their own."

"Is that a coincidence?" asked Azalea, a keen eye on the door and an ear alert to signs of human activity.

"Seems unlikely, doesn't it?" Teddy measured two new shots of gin into the cocktail shaker. "And not only were Algy and Bobo on hand for the proceedings, so was Portion."

"Portion?"

"Portia Beanfield — called Portion because she may be in this room with us as we speak. She might, in fact, be in your purse as we speak. She also, of course, has no motive, unless she's a kleptomaniac." Teddy added one level eyeful of lime cordial. "I'll note, for instance, there was a whole bowl of smidgen shrimp here earlier. Not pointing any fingers, but facts are facts."

Teddy rained ice shards into the shaker and closed it.

"Our next contestant is the charming and debonair Major Stanley Longrave, who was also at The Hollows — the Woolpit's bloodsport mud fort — when the first heist occurred." Teddy paused to indulge the cocktail shaker in its calling. "But he has the opposite of a motive to steal the necklace — he already stole it once, and he's convinced that stealing this particular gem brings bad luck."

"Is that everyone?"

"Unless you did it." Teddy poured two more gimlets. "The staff are in the clear just because if they were ever going to steal the necklace they wouldn't have waited until it was locked in a safe, which actually brings us to the most vexing aspect of this heist — it's impossible."

"Well, very evidently, dear, it isn't," observed Azalea.

"No, fair enough, obviously not," acknowledged Teddy. "But Topsy — Lord Turville — is sure that nobody else knew the combination to the safe and he takes the further precaution of changing it weekly. He'd rotated it just before guests starting arriving this weekend."

"What good fortune." Azalea sipped her fizz. "This is very nice. Tangy."

"Thank you. Good fortune? What's good fortune?"

"I was referring to the fact that the robbery appears to be impossible."

"Yes, lucky break, that." Teddy toasted this happy turn of affairs. "How is it good fortune?"

"I merely mean to say that in the absence of a viable suspect, the next best thing is to work out how it was done, which will doubtless lead you to the guilty party." Azalea paused her coupe mid-journey. "Oh, I say, Teddy — you're not going to have to call the police, are you? You know I can't bear the company of strangers."

"Can't call the rozzers, as it happens," said Teddy. "The gem's not insured, and Topsy doesn't know that. I not only have to work out who did it, I have to get it back, all without anyone knowing it was ever gone."

"I'm most reassured." Azalea, calmer now, nevertheless took the precaution of finishing her gin gimlet in a single throw. "One other thing, Teddy — why do you have a penguin?"

"To which penguin do you refer, Aunty A?" Teddy regarded Tuxedo Bird, who was dancing with his reflection in the glass panes of the French doors. "Ah. That penguin. That's Tuxedo Bird, he's…"

Teddy, too, finished her drink in a gulp of epiphany. "...he's just worked out how the necklace was stolen."

CHAPTER SIX

Which addresses the importance of precision when stealing jewellery and barns.

Aunty Azalea's anxiety threshold for attending foredinner drinks, it turns out, is four gin gimlets. The last two were generous overpours, however, so the usual clinical trial qualifiers apply.

"No one's here yet," observed Teddy. Aunty Azalea had made the observation of the otherwise empty drawing room, only sooner and silently and with joy in her heart.

Teddy opened the French doors to the interior garden.

"Now, I just need to recall where everyone was when Midgeham announced dinner."

At that moment, as though sprung from a trap, Midgeham appeared with the machines of martini.

"Excellent timing, Midgeham," welcomed Teddy. "Do you recall where everyone was standing yesterday when you announced dinner?"

"Yes, madame," replied the butler from somewhere deep in his nasal passages. "They were here, in the drawing room."

"I meant more precisely than that."

Midgeham took stock of his surroundings.

"His Lordship was there, where you are now, smoking his pipe."

"Excellent."

"Her Ladyship was next to him."

"Another direct hit, Midgely," encouraged Teddy. "Keep 'em coming."

"I regret, madame, that this is all I can recall with any certainty."

"Quite alright Midgerman. It's a solid starting point." Teddy paced the circumference of the room, stopping by the grand entrance, by which Midgeham departed. "What matters now is exactly where they were with respect to the angle of the French door."

"Why?" asked Azalea who, as a precaution, had stepped partially into the garden.

"That's how the thief got the combination to the safe," explained Teddy. "He watched Lord Topsy open it in the reflection. So, Aunty, when everyone comes in for drinks, you must remain where you are..."

"I could even go into the garden, if it would help," offered Azalea. "Or back to my room."

"I need you, following my subtle cues, to open the door to the same angle it was last night. Then you just wander casually over to the door of Topsy's office. From there, the person you see reflected in the glass of the garden door is the thief."

"But, what makes you think everyone will be in the same place they were last night?" asked, quite reasonably, Aunt Azalea.

"The psychology of the room," brazened Teddy. "Bobo was looking at himself in the mirror, Stilts was staying clear of the chandelier, Portion was taking cover next to him, and Algy was occupying the middle ground. The Woolpits were holding court in the only chairs in the room, as is to be expected, and Major Lonegrave was, oh, let's say, securing the perimeter." Teddy nodded in confident accord with her own assessment. "No, really, I have no idea. I'm hoping that as we circulate, the players will, at some point, be positioned as they were last night. That's why you have to be ready by the French doors."

"I think it would be best for all concerned, Teddy, if someone else were to do it."

"I have it on good authority, Auntsy, that I can trust no one."

"Oh, dear." Aunty Azalea, with the cool cunning of a seasoned mercenary, inventoried the exits and cover, including a generously accommodating rubber plant, as the other house guests filtered into the drawing room.

Stilts Stollery led the party, ducking under the door frame wearing a white dinner jacket that made him look just a bit like Mont Blanc from the Italian side. He was followed by Beauregard Pilewright who had elected tonight to favour the locals with a crimson satin cummerbund and matching bowtie, briefly giving Aunt Azalea the hope that he might distract the assembly by producing a rabbit from his hat. Teddy handed out gin martinis that she poured from a pitcher, having had the foresight to manufacture them in bulk.

Portion Beanfield wandered in next, after first bouncing off the door jamb and then the rubber plant, to which she apologised, and then Teddy. She had dressed for dinner in a silver ball gown and brocade matador's jacket that didn't match in the slightest.

Algy Brookbridge followed. He wore the same tuxedo he'd worn the night before, but was now affecting to fiddle with the jacket as an aide to masking the fact that the button had popped off when he tried to do it up while coming down the stairs.

As each guest arrived perfunctory presentations were made of Aunty Azalea, who smiled gamely and occasionally managed a subtly but solidly inapt laugh, giving the universal impression that she was a hopeless but harmless drunk.

Sir Oswald and Lady Dorothea Woolpit negotiated the doorway next, both in green velvet that did not work well as a tuxedo, unless compared to how well it worked as an evening gown. They were followed by Major Lonegrave in black dinner jacket, stiff shirtfront with white silk butterfly tie, and Thai fishing trousers.

Finally Lord and Lady Turville joined the buoyant little cocktail party. Topsy was in mathematically boring evening everything and Lady Turville was in black satin with a belt and bandolier formed of a trunk-to-tail parade of silver elephants. She also had little elephant earrings and her tiara was a depiction in gold and platinum relief of Hannibal crossing the Alps.

And the players were all back on the board. Teddy cast Azalea a sly wink, but it was difficult to say if her aunt caught it. One of the key practices of those trying not to be noticed is trying not to take notice. Azalea stared straight ahead, still and unseeing, like a bust of Beethoven struck on the back of the head with a wrench.

Habit and habitat are powerful forces, particularly when met with no resistance, and soon enough Teddy identified a clear point in the game when all the pieces were positioned just as they'd been the previous night when Lord Turville took his wife's necklace into the office.

Teddy herself had been talking to Beauregard, who smiled at her now as she poured him a gin martini.

"My heart is thirsty for that noble pledge. Fill, Teddy, *till the wine o'erswell the cup."*

"Julius Caesar," identified Teddy. "Again."

"Is it?"

Aunty Azalea stood by the French doors which were angled such that they revealed nothing at all. Teddy issued a subtle wave. Azalea stared straight ahead. Teddy cleared her throat. Azalea focused hard on some vexing puzzle playing out in the middle field. Teddy spoke up.

"How many of those gin martinis have you had, Aunty? You remember what happened on our trip to Deauville." Teddy confided quietly to the entire room, "She absolutely insisted on flying the plane which, obviously, they couldn't let her do, chiefly because we were on a boat. In the end they just let her wear the captain's hat and she calmed right down."

Azalea laughed a silvery, sweet, lightly deranged laugh, and Teddy had her attention. She didn't so much follow Teddy's frantic series of winks and waves, precisely, but rather she slowly opened and closed the door until something different happened.

And then something different happened. Teddy saw Stilts in the reflection of the glass, smiling that vacant, hopelessly hopeful smile.

She held up a halt hand, and knew that the door was angled just as it was the previous night. She looked around the room. One of those present was angled to see into Lord Turville's office via the reflection in the window. She gave the sign to Azalea, but Azalea had abandoned her post, and was affecting to examine the leaves of the rubber plant as a pretext for hiding behind it.

So Teddy walked her pitcher of martinis around the room, topping up glasses and sending her aunt telepathic notes of censure and regret which, thankfully, cannot be repeated here. When she'd finally worked her way into position at the door to Topsy's office, she was able to turn her attention to the reflection in the glass, between her and which stood Midgeham announcing, "Dinner is served."

"No." Teddy said this with the tone and tenor with which people shout 'fire!' "Nobody move. I mean to say, I want to remember everyone just as they are. Except you, Midgeham, I'd like to remember you over there, by the door. Yes. Much better."

Finally, Teddy could look squarely at the French windows, angled exactly as they were last night when the thief saw reflected there the combination to the safe. There in the glass, smiling back at her, was Algy Brookbridge.

❦

"Algernon Brookbridge did not steal any necklace."

Topsy Turville made this sweeping declaration to Teddy and Glitz in a low voice behind the thick doors of his office, to which they'd absconded after dinner under pretext of an emergency tie straightening.

"Very well, then, Lord Turville," challenged Teddy. "Then how do you explain the fact that he did it?"

"He didn't."

"He did," parried Teddy. "He's the only one who could have."

72

"By watching me turn the combination in the reflection in the window?" scorned Topsy. "Teddy, it's absurd."

"He has excellent eyesight and a photographic memory for details, numbers, and poetry," barristered Teddy, "just like Dick Turpin."

"Young lady, you are meant to be selecting one of these gentlemen to marry," instructed Lord Turville. "Not accusing them of theft."

"My dear Lord Turville, I'm a grown woman with a degree from Oxford," countered Teddy. "I'm quite capable of doing two things at once. In any case, I'm not accusing them of anything, I'm only accusing Algy, and even then — note the careful observation of convention — because he did it."

"Talk to her, Gladys," exasperated Topsy.

"We can't accuse a guest of stealing," agreed Glitz. "Can't you find someone else to accuse?"

"You accused me," pointed out Teddy. "Almost immediately, in fact."

"Well, it's the sort of thing you do, Teddy," defended Glitz. "You stole Baron Milsip's barn."

"I did not steal Baron Milsip's barn," disdained Teddy. "I had it moved to his duck island, on account of him calling Papa a brick."

"That's a good thing," said Topsy. "A brick is a solid chap."

"Yes, I know that, now. I was eleven at the time."

For years, Lord Turville had played county cricket, and he knew the value of a strong appeal to authority. Nevertheless, he took a crack at it.

"Gladdy, I know how much that necklace meant to you, and I'm very sorry."

"Yes…" Glitz's wane smile was interpreted by Topsy as melancholy.

"After the weekend we can involve the police and make a claim on the insurance," Topsy said consolingly. "And then you can have another one made, exactly like the old one." To Teddy, His Lordship addressed a loving aside, "She designed it herself, you know."

Teddy caught Glitz's glassy eye and rigid smile, not unlike those assumed by Aunt Azalea when she's attempting to pass for scenery. Nevertheless, there was deep pathos and meaning behind her frozen countenance, and a silent but substantial psychic scream.

"Right oh, Tops," mollified Teddy. "If you're happy to harbour a jewel thief right here in Hardy Hall, I suppose that's your prerogative as host."

"There now," exhaled Topsy. "Much better."

"I'll just return to the business of selecting a husband." Teddy touched a definitive hand to a decisive doorknob. "I say, wouldn't it be an absolute caution if it turned out to be Algy? I expect I'd make a dashed fine helpmeet for a career criminal. While he's off, doing a stretch at Dartmoor, I could be at home with Mama's grandchildren, instructing them in artisanal forgery."

Glitz flounced nervously after Teddy with a deliberate spontaneity, if that's not an oxymoron, which it is. They walked in silence to a dark and quiet corner of the hall.

"What are we going to do, Teddy?"

"We know he took it," said Teddy. "You don't fancy just asking him to give it back?"

"What if he denies it?"

"The recommended procedure is matchsticks between the toes, but I take it you'd prefer something more subtle."

"Please."

"Old place like this, there ought to be an iron maiden on the premises."

"Teddy…" Glitz idled with her bandolier, picking up reflected moon beams in the ruby eyes of a baby elephant. "Please try to think of something."

"Already have, Glads," Teddy assured her. "I'm going to nick it back."

"Steal it from his room?"

"Well, no, in that it's not stealing, but, yes, in that it stands to reason that it's in his room. He's unlikely to be wearing it."

"But what if you're caught?" fretted Glitz.

"I plan to mitigate that risk, Glitz, by not getting caught," answered Teddy with the easy confidence of privileged youth. "Which is Algy's room?"

"First floor, north-west corner. It's above the library."

"Right. The boys will still be in the games room, trying to outdrink and outsnooker one another," calculated Teddy. "Try to keep them there as long as you can. I may need to search a bit."

"He'll have locked his room, surely. I can ask Midgeham for the key."

"No, you can't," differed Teddy, "because he'll tell Topsy who only minutes ago forbade us from investigating the guests. Besides, who locks their rooms in a country house?"

"Jewel thieves?" suggested Glitz.

"Ah, but we have the advantage, Lady Gladys — he doesn't know that we know he's a jewel thief."

※

From thence events unfolded in trim shims of tight timing.

Teddy took the main stairs to the first floor. Simultaneously Glitz, feigning a casual gait, worked her way to the games room.

Achieving the first floor which was, as expected, dark and deserted, Teddy moved noiselessly down the hall, arriving at the door to the north-west corner suite four seconds later. At that same moment, Glitz reached the door of the games room.

Teddy entered Algy's suite and Glitz entered the games room.

Algy's room was empty. So was the games room.

Teddy took systematic stock — valise, wardrobe, dresser, writing desk, followed by whatever was in the bedroom, the door of which was currently closed.

Glitz kneaded her fingers and emitted a soft whine.

Teddy set about her search, starting with the wardrobe.

Glitz continued to wring her hands, but she had the whining largely under control.

The valise contained a sock. The wardrobe contained only a man's wardrobe. Teddy deprioritised the top of the wardrobe until she found something to stand on.

Glitz, in a fit and flurry of decisive action, left the games room.

Teddy searched the writing desk. It contained writing desk things.

Now in the hall, Glitz finally realised that Algy must be in his room.

Teddy opened the bedroom door of Algy's room.

Glitz resumed emitting an anxious whine.

Teddy snapped on the bedroom light, and instantly heard "What ho, Algy."

In the hall, at the door which Teddy had left open, was Portion.

"Oh, what ho, Portion," replied Teddy with the ease that comes from years of fabricating extemporaneous cover stories. "Have you seen Tuxedo Bird? Can't find him anywhere."

Portion, for her part, was still processing the anomaly of hearing Teddy's voice from the blob that she assumed to be Algernon Brookbridge. She put on her glasses.

"Teddy? What are you doing here?"

Weak as it obviously was, Teddy was about to double down on the missing penguin pretext when Algy stepped in through the balcony doors, holding a book of poetry.

"Oh," said Portion in accordance with the construction she put on the situation.

"Portia?" Algy performed an almost flawless triple-take between the hall and bedroom doorways. "Teddy?"

"Forgive me." Portion pivoted on her heel like an honour guard and marched off down the hall.

"Uh oh." Algy assumed a sheepish air. "Do you think she'll tell?"

"Tell what?" wondered Teddy.

"Well, that you were in my room." Algy appraised the scene. "What are you doing in my room, by the way?"

"Looking for my penguin."

"In my room?"

"I thought it was Portion's," claimed Teddy. "She's grown quite attached to Tuxedo Bird."

"Oh, right." Algy reflected on this. "I should tell her that."

"I wouldn't." Teddy approached and spoke in confidential tones. "Frankly, Tuxedo Bird finds her a little clingy."

"I mean that I'd explain that you thought this was her room." Algy appeared to notice that he was carrying a book of romantic poetry, which he then put quickly behind his back. "I'm just thinking of your reputation."

"I don't know why you should. I never do."

"Nevertheless…"

"Oh, all right, Algy," acquiesced Teddy. "I'll handle it."

"Would you?"

"In my inimitable way." Teddy took a turn about the room, "This is a very nice little arrangement," and observed in the mirror the grey metal lid of a lockbox on top of the wardrobe, "These corner rooms are always so much brighter," then she calculated the likelihood that Algy would in future lock his room, "Do you find heating an issue?" so she stepped out the French doors, "Does this balcony wrap around?" and observed that the west wall water spout curved over Algy's window, past his balcony, and drained into the moat next to that of the library, one floor below.

❦

"Algy has taken to locking his door."

Teddy announced this inevitability to the wardrobe in which Aunty Azalea was hiding.

"That was probably to be expected," replied the wardrobe.

"No, I know. It just feels I let an easy opportunity go to waste, like that time I saw Oswald Mosely bending over the rails of Macclesfield Bridge."

The wardrobe considered this. Teddy opened the balcony doors so Tuxedo Bird could waddle in.

"You could ask Midgeham for the key," proposed the wardrobe.

"No, I couldn't, because he'd at the very least tell Topsy, and even then he probably wouldn't give it to me." Teddy opened the wardrobe to reveal Azalea sitting on a hat box, knitting. "Besides, I have a better plan, much more in keeping with my talents."

"Blackmail, dear?"

"My other talents," specified Teddy, "there's no time for subtlety. No, I shall effect a perfectly planned and executed recovery — a counter-heist."

CHAPTER SEVEN

*In which the composure of a country house is tested, and Portion
destroys the evidence.*

Teddy, dressed in black pyjamas with an orange tiger embroidered
on the back, moved from column to door to column down the dark
hall to the library. Somewhere, a clock struck eleven.

The library door squealed like a teacher's pet. Teddy froze and
listened for predators. The moment passed and she carefully closed
the door behind her.

She paused for a beat and then was padding towards the balcony
doors when she heard "Who's there?" to which she quickly and
calmly replied "Gah!"

"Teddy?"

"Portion?" Teddy asked the silhouette framed by the fading
embers in the fireplace. "What are you doing here in the dark?"

"Oh. Just... staying out of the way." Portion said this with a
tortured sigh, like a woman deciding between another round and
throwing herself off Westminster Bridge. "I'm sorry I intruded on
you and Algy."

"Piff. It's nothing," dismissed Teddy. "We're very casual. I still
haven't told him my parents are alive."

"So, you haven't settled on him, then?" Portion flicked a paper
pea into the embers of the evening fire. "Or do you propose to keep
all three off the market indefinitely?"

In case the attitude behind these remarks was unclear, Portion
followed them with another sigh.

"I thought you didn't care for Algy." Teddy wandered over to the
fire and took the odeon seat across from Portion. "You called him a
big dumb rock."

"So he is a big dumb rock."

"I see." Teddy watched Portion flick two more paper balls into the miniature inferno. "Glitz tells me that you have a chap on the hook in London. Want to tell me about him?"

"Not awfully, no."

"Anything like Algernon Brookbridge, at all?" asked Teddy.

"Not even a little. He's very kind and very loyal and in every possible way the precise opposite of Algy Brookbridge." Portion emphasised 'Algy' and 'Brook' and 'bridge' with three more paper missiles into paper pea purgatory.

"Then I suppose you don't want to know what I was really doing in his room."

"I'm very sure that it's none of my business, Teddy," sniffed Portion. "And at any rate I know exactly what you were doing in his room."

"Right oh."

Portion sighed in a manner contrived to convey disinterest, but a sigh is always a poor choice of vehicle for conveying disinterest.

"I didn't know he was there," said Teddy.

"I see."

"I thought he was in the games room, with the other boys." Teddy almost always builds a story on a grain of truth, if there's one handy. "I went to his room to put purple food dye in his tooth powder."

"Where did you get purple food dye?"

"My dear Portion, when would I ever weekend in a country house without a full stock of purple food dye?"

Portion's suspicious squint was almost entirely wasted in the dark.

"Why did you put purple food dye in Algy's tooth powder?"

"Well, not that I'm casting blame, Ports, but I didn't. I was interrupted."

"Then why were you going to?" clarified Portion.

"It's part of a larger strategy to get him to ask my mother to withdraw his candidacy for the role of son-in-law," extemporised Teddy. "The first shot over the bow, if you will."

"Were you going to put purple food dye in all the boys' tooth powder?" marvelled Portion. "Tonight?"

"Obviously not, Portion," scoffed Teddy. "No, Algy was food dye in the tooth powder, Bobo was going to get an alarm clock hidden up his chimney and set for four in the morning, and I was undecided if I was going to put Tuxedo Bird in Stilts' bath or set all his shoes out to be polished which, if I'm honest, strikes me as a trifle elementary. In fact, I think I left him shoeless last summer when we all drove down to Brighton."

"You did." Portion tossed a paper pea into the air like a tennis ball and then served it with the back of her hand into the depth of the fire. "He rolled up his trouser legs and confined himself to the beach."

"Oh, that's right," recalled Teddy, fondly. "I really must work up some sort of filing system. What's that you're throwing into the fire, Ports?"

"Nothing of any significance."

"Come along, Portion, you can't think I'd betray a friend, can you?" disdained Teddy. "Obviously I know that you and Algy are sweethearts."

"Of course we're not sweethearts."

"You two should synchronise your stories," advised Teddy. "Algy told me he hadn't met you until yesterday, but you told me that you met him during the shooting weekend at the Woolpits'."

"Oh, right."

"And then of course there were your ham-handed efforts to put me off him," said Teddy. "Big dumb rock, indeed. You clearly put no spirit into that — it was you who gave Stilts his nickname and got the entire upper fifth at St Swithun's to refer to Miss Firmstone, the PE mistress, as Piltdown Ma'am."

"She inspired me," reminisced Portion. "Something about that eyebrow…"

"Precisely my point," said Teddy in her summation. "So, returning to the question of biblioclasm…"

Portion regarded the ruins in her hands with dismay. "It's Algy's last letter to me."

"Was he trying out a new pet name?" asked Teddy. "You'll want to take my advice and always keep those on file, to be recited among friends on special occasions."

"It's okay." She held up the shreds. "Really it was just the envelope. But you were in his room, and you went for a very long walk on the island."

"Yes, what about that?" complained Teddy. "Why did Mama throw Algy into the ring if he's already gone down for the count?"

"It was Lord Turville who invited him."

"That's hardly the point. He didn't have to come."

"He did, in fact," maintained Portion. "Nobody knows about us. It's why Algy had to play along when Lord Turville invited him down for the weekend."

"When you say Lord Turville, you mean the man himself?"

"Literally an engraved invitation."

"But, why not just refuse?" Teddy needed to know. "Why all the subterfuge and sub rosa when you could just take him off the market and reduce my workload by a third?"

Portion resumed her practice of sighing. "Algy's father doesn't approve of me."

"Blimey," gogged Teddy. "What can you possibly have done? Algy's father approves of *me*."

"It's not me to whom he objects, exactly," pouted Portion. "It's Papa."

"Who could possibly object to Busby Beanfield?" wondered Teddy. "Doesn't he volunteer at the zoo?"

"Yes. He's on the reptile board and petting committee."

"And isn't there a dog shelter named for him in Greenwich?"

"Beanfield Green Field," confirmed Portion. "He put up the initial funding plus an annuity."

"Is Algy's father a cat man?"

"He thinks Papa has no head for business."

"Has he?"

"Not at all." Portion idly folded a complex construction from a bit of envelope. "There's very little margin in giving your money to dog shelters."

"You surprise me." Teddy considered this revelation. "Unless I've got the wrong end of this stick altogether, though, it's his own money he's giving away, and not that of Algy's father. Is that the rough state of affairs?"

"Correct."

"Right oh, then. So, at the risk of exposing my own financial shortcomings, what bizwit is it of his?"

"Abernathy Brookbridge just generally objects to people using their wealth for something other than amassing more wealth." Portion launched the folded paper construction, which turned out to be an aeroplane, toward the fire, where it met a tragic end. "But more specifically, Beanfield Green Field is on a plot of land on which Mister Brookbridge had planned to build a glue factory, on account of its unique position straddling Deptford Creek, which apparently makes it very convenient for shipping, storage, and dumping effluence into the river. Papa outbid him."

"He just outright bid more for the property? On the open market?" awed Teddy. "What is your papa, some sort of communist?"

"He might just as well be so far as Abernathy Brookbridge is concerned," sighed Portion. "He says he'll cut Algy off without a penny if he even mentions the name Beanfield to him again."

"I see."

"Not quite, you don't, Tedds…" They were sitting in the dark in the middle of the night in an otherwise empty room but, nevertheless, Portion lowered her voice and leaned towards Teddy and in general instituted the protocols of the shared scarlet secret. "The fact is, Teddy…"

"That Algy has a plan."

"He does." Portion withdrew from the zone of secrecy. "How did you know?"

"I have an intuition for these things," said Teddy. "It tells me that Algy's found some way of getting around his father's threat to impoverish him."

"That's right, he has."

"I think he might need a backup plan, Portion."

"Why do you say that?"

"Another intuition. Once they start they just keep on coming." Teddy stood and stretched yawningly. "All reassured now about me and Algy?"

"Yes, thanks Tedds. Are you still going to put purple food dye in his tooth powder?"

"I can't be shown to be playing favourites, Porch."

"No, of course." Portion picked up on the subtle stretch and yawn, and skipped happily towards the door, where she stopped. "You're not going to bed?"

"I just came to get a book."

"What book?"

"Not sure..." Teddy surveyed four walls of floor-to-ceiling shelves. "Something with fish in it. Tuxedo Bird wants a bedtime story."

"Right oh, good night Tedds."

The drain pipe on the west wall of Hardy Hall empties into the moat next to the library balcony. From there it rises past Algy's balcony, takes a left, and then heads up to the roof where it convenes with the gutters. The roof was heavy with a wet mantle of snow that had fallen during the day, and now the snow had stopped and the temperature had turned enough for it to be rapidly melting and for the drain pipe to be actively earning its keep.

Teddy stepped up onto the balustrade and took hold of the pipe. It was cold and slippery and it jiggled. Slick spatters of slush sluiced from the roof and splotched on Teddy's face. Thusly encouraged, she fitted a foot into a mortar joint and tested the strength of the pipe. It held, so she put another foot into another joint, one granite block higher, and heaved.

Now she was a full Teddy above the balcony but only about half-a-Teddy over it. The other half, were it to look down, would see the black, icy waters of the moat. She stepped up the height of one more granite block.

Upstairs, in his room in his bed in the middle of the exciting bit of Byron's *Childe Harold's Pilgrimage,* Algy thought he heard something. To tear away the layers of uncertainty, he did hear something, but he remained unsure until he heard it again, much louder. It started as a dubious, trepidant creaking, as of a rusty hinge that's really quite embarrassed by its outburst. Then it grew almost instantly more extroverted and then positively hysterical, until the sound was of a great rending of iron and planning. This all ended with an explosive 'sploosh' which quickly softened into the gentle wash and woosh of running water, as of a brook or forest creek or ruptured water spout.

In the urgency of the moment Algy threw off the bedclothes and very nearly forgot to bookmark Byron before splashing to the balcony doors and flinging them open. The spout had come away from the wall, as though bodily pulled by some force below. Algy peered over his balcony and saw only the drain, warped and buckled, yawing over the cold, still waters of the moat.

The pipe, however, had parted ways with the gutters at the join above Algy's balcony, and the waters flooding his room were anything but still. They flowed in with a healthy, happy abandon, bubbling and babbling and certain of their welcome.

❦

It's the very rarity of upheavals in the routine of a country great house that makes them such a treat. Everyone turns out, for one thing, and there's a chummy easing of the normal social boundaries among residents brought together in their pyjamas.

His Lordship, for example, was the first to respond to Algy's confused shouts of 'flood!', which he'd adapted from what he believed to be the advised procedure in case of fire. Topsy had only time to throw on a dressing gown, tie off the belt, even out and centre the bow, and comb his hair before racing hell-for-leather into the hall. He was followed by Glitz who, happily, was already wearing her best night necklace.

Stilts arrived next with a nasty welt on his forehead from knocking it on the top of his bedroom door and then, again, seconds later, the top of the hall door. He was followed by Beauregard who, in his haste, had matched a burgundy housecoat with a burgundy ascot.

Even the maids, the cook, and the footmen arrived before Midgeham, who had taken the time to fully dress in accordance with his unshakeable certainty that there never has been and never will be an exigency under his jurisdiction that warrants running, shouting, or incorrect attire.

It was from this point onwards that order resumed its reign. Midgeham put the maids onto the task of rolling up the carpet into a serviceable sea patch and the footmen to work moving Algy's affairs to the first alternate guest room. Everyone pitched in. Lady Turville poured out the brandy and the men drank it, and even Aunty Azalea, hiding behind a planter column, discreetly advised and directed the footmen as they recreated Algy's room, two doors over.

More brandy was drunk. More slush melted from the roof and fell past the windows to sploosh into the moat. Everyone went to bed and most went to sleep, but in Teddy's room Tuxedo Bird stood at the balcony doors, staring at and studying the waters of the moat and knowing, in a firm but foggy penguin sort of way, that something was not as it should be. Somewhere, a clock struck four.

In Algy's new room the steamer trunk that the footmen had struggled into place by the wardrobe bumped, gave voice to a hoarse but heartfelt 'ow', and then slowly opened. Teddy unfolded out of the trunk, closed it, stepped up onto it so that she could reach down the lockbox from the top of the wardrobe, and did so.

Happily, Algy had continued the widely observed tradition of leaving the key in the lock on the inside, and with much relief Teddy unlocked the door and left. Plan B had been spending the remainder of the night in the trunk.

"What ho, Aunty, Tux," whispered Teddy on return to her room. Tuxedo Bird expressed his relief in clumsy but convivial flaps of his wings. Aunty Azalea started from a strategic slumber she'd instituted behind the divan.

Teddy put the lockbox on the cocktail table. "Like a clockwork shop clerk — efficient and effective and little to no breakage."

"Only somewhat extensive water damage," noted Azalea in her library, killjoy voice.

"Topsy won't object to that once he realises he's got the necklace back without spilling a drop of decorum." Teddy examined the lockbox from several angles. "Have you an axe, Aunty?"

"I have a darning needle."

"Very close," said Teddy. "Practically interchangeable, unless one is showing a maitre d' that one means business, or doing whatever it is one does with darning needles. You're not saying you can pick a lock."

"How do you mean, pick a lock?" asked Azalea. "Do you mean select a specific one from a range of similar locks?"

"I do not." Teddy scanned the room, settling on a pair of candle holders on the mantelpiece. But even while Teddy was testing the heft of a brass pipe, Azalea was applying a darning needle to the lockbox.

"It's often much simpler to simply slip the posts out of the hinges of a box like this." She held up two slim pins.

"Well, that's handy to know." Teddy sat on the divan next to Aunty Azalea. "However did you come to work that out?"

"Puckeridge — he's head of staff…"

"Yes, I recall old Puckers," said Teddy. "He's your butler."

"That's him. He keeps the liquor cabinet locked," explained Azalea. "It has hinges much like these."

"Aunty, he's your butler," pointed out Teddy. "You can just ask him to open it. In fact, you can tell him to open it and mix the entire contents into a salad bowl and serve it with a ladle."

"I don't like to bother him." Azalea took hold of the lid of the lockbox and loosened it with a little shake. "Shall we see this necklace?"

"You might want to prepare yourself," warned Teddy. "It's a difficult piece and open to interpretation. Taken in the right spirit, it might just give you a heretofore unknown appreciation for junk jewellery and vandalism."

Azalea raised the lid to reveal a layer of grey paper, which Teddy removed.

"Empty," grieved Teddy.

"What made you think it was in the box at all?" asked Azalea.

"It's the only place that made sense." Teddy unfolded the paper, in pursuit of the possibility that the necklace had shrunk. "Nothing else in the room locks, anywhere would risk..." She stopped unfolding. Teddy and Azalea looked at the tables and diagrams and title on the paper, and then they looked at each other, and said,

"The formula for Stickle."

CHAPTER EIGHT

In which is featured prominently the formula for Stickle.

"The formula for Stickle."

"The formula for Stickle?"

"The formula for Stickle."

This fertile exchange of ideas went from strength to strength the following morning, in the breakfast room, between Teddy and Lord Turville.

"Algy not only stole Glitz's ugly necklace, he somehow got hold of the formula for Stickle," Teddy assured him. "Was it in the safe too?"

"Theodora, I have precisely no idea what you're talking about." His Lordship, already dressed at seven-thirty in the morning in his banker's blues and barleycorn, was at the sideboard, arranging strips of bacon on his plate according to length. "What, if anything at all, is Stickle?"

"Your top-secret new glue which reportedly and, probably hyperbolically, can repair the wing of an aeroplane in flight." Teddy, less disposed in general to observing the niceties of breakfast and particularly so this morning, was in a kimono, indoor slippers and outdoor scarf, and she was drawing strength from a bowl of sweet black coffee.

"If such a thing existed, Teddy, and it was indeed top-secret," contended Lord Turville, "then it further stands to reason that you wouldn't know about it."

"Topsy, I first heard about Stickle from Freddy Hannibal-Pool at the prize-giving of a scavenger hunt," said Teddy. "And Freddy religiously restricts her sources of information to the back pages of *Track and Turf.* Stickle might be a super secret, but it's a super poorly-kept super secret."

Lord Turville reflected on this development as he idly exchanged the fried egg he'd selected for a more symmetrical model.

"How could this possibly have happened?"

"Have you not met Lady Dorothea Woolpit?" asked Teddy over a soup spoon of coffee.

Lord Turville considered this, aided in the effort by a good hard stare at his egg, and then concluded, "Ah."

"Coming to the light, Topsy?"

"It explains rather a lot, in fact." Lord Turville joined Teddy at the sunny end of the table, next to a window the height of a second dining room ceiling and offering a panorama of blue and white winter's morning. "Some weeks ago, Sir Oswald asked if he could invest in Stickle."

"There you go."

"And so did Tilden Stollery." Preoccupied, Topsy ate a rasher of bacon out of order. "And Major Lonegrave."

"How about the gardener?" asked Teddy. "You think he's still in the dark?"

"But, even if it was Lady Woolpit who told everyone about Stickle, how did she come to know about it?" Topsy idly bisected his egg into four equal parts.

"Gossips have powers beyond the ken of mortal men, Tops," explained Teddy. "Fairly Longway, one of the ladies of the auto club — seven litre SSK Roadster and an Austin Twelve for country driving — learned of her own parents' divorce in *Sighs and Whispers,* which is already quite an impressive act of gosspionage, but even her parents didn't know it at time of going to press. They thought they were perfectly happy."

"Yes, I see, Teddy…"

"They were planning a second honeymoon."

"Yes, Teddy, point taken."

"Happily…" Teddy swallowed a spoonful of coffee, "…they patched things up."

"The point being that Lady Woolpit has her sources, I understand," said Topsy.

"How many snares did you sell them?"

"You mean shares," corrected Topsy. "None. Stickle requires no further investment. Your father provided the development capital."

"Not Abernathy Brookbridge?" asked Teddy with a studied nonchalance.

The dining room door quietly opened at this point and Lady Turville slid through and closed it carefully behind her, as though she feared waking it up.

"What ho, Glitz," welcomed Teddy.

"Good morning." Glitz spoke in a weekend morning hush. It had been a trying night, and she'd dressed for calm and comfort in a quilted dressing gown and simple pearl necklace and bracelet string set with matching earrings and barrette. She approached the sideboard as though it was the edge of a cliff.

"Teddy's just been making the most extraordinary claim," announced Lord Turville.

"Oh, come along, Topsy, it's 1928," scolded Teddy. "People get divorced every day."

"She says that Algernon Brookbridge has stolen the formula for Stickle," said Topsy.

"Oh, dear." Glitz spotted and selected a frosted bun with pearl candy sprinkles. It visibly cheered her. She brought it to the table with a cup of coffee and sat and smiled at it. "What's Stickle, dear?"

"My top-secret glue project."

"I expect that's why I hadn't heard of it." Glitz spoke exactly like a woman stirring sugar and milk into her coffee and admiring her frosted bun. "Why does Teddy think that Algernon Brookbridge has your glue recipe?"

"Well, Glitz, what do you think all that strategic flooding was in aid of last night?" asked Teddy. "I used it as cover to get into Algy's room. I was looking for your necklace."

"Did you find it?" hoped Glitz.

"I did not," Teddy replied with considerable surprise. "He hid it somewhere else. Got the formula, though. You want it back, Tops?"

"Just a moment…" Topsy was struck by a grave thought while folding his bacon. "You have the formula?"

"I do and, no offence, it's a tough read — all show and no tell."

"You took it from Algy's room?" Topsy whispered this. They'd all been whispering to varying degrees throughout the conversation, but this was delivered with a professional whisper. A whisper that means business. "Does he know?"

"What is it, Tom?" Glitz picked up on her husband's tense sense.

"Topsy's concerned that Algy knows that I have the formula for Stickle," explained Teddy. "Because Topsy arranged for Algy to steal it."

❦

Algy awoke from a nightmare about waterfalls, for some reason.

He untangled himself from the bedclothes which, like Algy-clothes, weren't designed for a man built like a suit of mediaeval armour. He wrapped himself in a travel-weary but tough-minded terry cloth dressing gown and went to his reception room where he paused at the balcony windows to appreciate the complete absence of floodwaters. On the contrary, the morning was bright and crisp and clear, apart from a very light mist rising from the moat, beyond which the island gardens of Hardy Holm scintillated with that brittle layer of glitter formed of a light, wet snowfall which has since frozen.

He went to the wardrobe and took from it a towel. What he didn't do, it would have been welcome to know in the second dining room at that very moment, was look up and see that his lockbox was gone. Instead he went back to the bedroom to recover his book of poetry, with the intention of reading it in the bath.

This, however, gave Algy inspiration. He sat at the little writing desk, looking very much like a sixth-former who'd been held back twelve years, and put pen to paper.

'My dearest darling dove,'

An excellent start. Portion was fond of animals in general and birds in particular.

'Can't tell you how much it grieves me to have to hide like this. I adore that you came to my room last night but it's for the best that we were interrupted or I'd have soon had you in my arms and might have never let you go.'

Algy read it back and found it quick, clever, and coherent, with a clear and unambiguous message. He folded the note and returned to the path to the bath. As he passed the wardrobe he glanced up and, once again to what would have been much rejoicing in the breakfast room, had they only known, Algy failed to notice that the lockbox wasn't there. He did, however, have another thought regarding the note — it yet needed that small drop of ink, as Byron put it, as to make millions think. He returned to the writing desk.

'Always thinking of you, my...'

Algy stopped himself in the nick of time, for he was about to write 'my button bride' when he remembered how sensitive Portion was about her height. Button, flattering as it obviously is in almost every way, implies a certain diminutive stature. Musing on the problem, Algy settled his eyes on the wardrobe, and his gaze glided upward until...

'...statuesque bride.'

Much better, Algy thought, incorrectly. He read over the letter, found it wanting of nothing more, and signed it, 'With love, Algy'.

He reflected on what he'd written with particular consideration given over to how it would be received and, for that matter, delivered. He allowed his eyes to wander the room, as an aid to separating author from oeuvre, and noticed something missing. He immediately realised what it was, and so added 'PS, I shall place this under your pillow so that you'll know that I was here in your room.'

Once again he folded the letter and put it in his pocket and set out for the door. On the way, he looked up and saw that the lockbox was missing.

❧

"What could possibly make you think that I arranged for Algernon Brookbridge to steal the formula for Stickle?" Lord Turville wanted to know.

"Well, for one thing, you provided him with the combination to the safe."

"I did not give Algy the combination to my safe."

"No, you showed it to him," agreed Teddy. "Leveraging his exceptional memory and eyesight, you angled the French doors to the garden such that he could see into your office. Then you made a great public announcement of putting Glitz's necklace into the safe."

"Is this one of your famous constructions, Teddy?" Topsy, the picture of composure at the sideboard, filled a cup with seven parts coffee, one and third parts sugar, and two parts milk. "Like when you told that reporter for *The Times* that Shaw based *Pygmalion* on a weekend with your parents?"

"Got them invited to the palace, though, didn't it?" defended Teddy. "I've also learned, Topsy, that it wasn't my mother who conscripted Algy for bachelor duty this weekend — you invited him."

"Why would I arrange for someone to steal the formula for Stickle?" reasoned Topsy.

"Well, that I don't know, Tops," confessed Teddy. "Let's ask someone who does — Topsy, why would you arrange for someone to steal the formula for Stickle? There's no point denying it — you invited Algy here even though his father helped develop Stickle and might have cause to believe that he's been cut out of his share of the riches, then you provided him opportunity and means to... oh my antsy aunty, Stickle doesn't work."

"Well, of course it works, Teddy." Lord Turville spoke with conviction but his actions betrayed him — he over-stirred his coffee and was obliged to start over. "It's just that it works a trifle too well."

"Can glue work too well?"

"I mean to say, Stickle doesn't stop working," explained Topsy. "The remarkable characteristic of Stickle, that which makes it a wholesale improvement over any competing adhesive, is that it bonds equivalent — and only equivalent — molecular structures. Metal to metal, china plate to shard of china plate, that sort of thing. It does so by breaking down the respective molecular bodies and then rebinding them as a solid singularity."

"I assumed as much," lied Teddy.

"The problem with Stickle is that it doesn't stop at the damaged surface," continued Topsy. "Over time — rather a short time, it turns out — it dissolves the entire object."

"I could imagine certain practical applications for that," said Teddy. "But yes, I see the problem. So my father's investment is lost?"

"As matters stand now, yes," doomed Topsy. "He financed all of the development costs, even when they grew rather exponentially after the problem was first identified."

"Without getting into actual numbers which, frankly, bore me, how much money is at stake?" asked Teddy. "Put it on a sliding scale from Vicky the Finicky Four Litre to the family estate in Berkshire, with my flat in Chelsea indicating the median."

"Teddy, it's as bad as it can possibly be." Topsy failed to mix another cup of coffee with anything like precision but, so complete was his distraction, he sat and drank it.

"Stickle is going to ruin my family?" ghasted Teddy. "Surely there's something that can be done."

Topsy regarded Teddy with a flat yet meaningful gaze.

"Something was done, Teddy," he said. "You undid it."

"Oh."

"Algy's father, Abernathy Brookbridge, joined the project late last year," narrated Topsy with a soupçon of reproach. "He agreed to compensate your father for his entire investment, plus a ten percent royalty on future profits, but then, quite suddenly, he retracted the offer."

"Because he knew that Stickle didn't work?"

"No, at the time we all believed that it did work," corrected Topsy. "Abernathy Brookbridge only joined the project so that he could steal the formula, which he did."

"Hang on, Tops — you're saying that Brookbridge already has the formula?" niggled Teddy.

"Yes."

"Then what's the point in Algy stealing it?"

"Brookbridge discovered, doubtless about the same time we did, that Stickle didn't work or, as I say, worked too well," said Topsy. "So, to tempt him back to the table, we let it be known that we'd solved the problem, and that there was a new formula."

"But you didn't solve the problem."

"No, and in any case Brookbridge refused to negotiate," Topsy brooded over his imperfect coffee.

"But didn't you have a contract?" Glitz asked this. She had maintained a mainly spectator role while she ate the pearl candies off all the frosted buns. Having completed that business, she took a more active interest in the sinkhole of her family finances.

"We had a verbal agreement," clarified Topsy. "The intention was to formalise matters after due diligence, but Brookbridge used the opportunity to steal the formula."

"Is a verbal agreement not worth anything?" hoped Teddy.

"It is, if we can prove it was made, and that the terms were fulfilled." His Lordship examined his spoon for flaws and appeared to find several. "By stroke of luck, I accidentally recorded the initial agreement on my dictaphone."

"So now you need only prove that Brookbridge has the formula," deduced Teddy.

"Which is what I was trying to do."

Glitz sought clarification on a point of order, "How does letting it be stolen a second time accomplish that?"

"He changed the formula in some key way," said Teddy.

"We added galacturonic acid," confirmed Topsy.

"I see." Teddy issued a slyly wily nod of entirely false comprehension.

"Pectin?" Glitz, as it happened, was in that moment pouring a pot of her homemade forest berry jam, which had become mainly runny purple juice and lumps of red currant, onto a bun.

"Pectin," said Topsy. "It makes little difference what we selected, so long as it could be identified in laboratory analysis."

"And how are you going to manage that?" asked Teddy.

"We have a man inside Brookbridge Industrial Adhesives," confided Topsy. "If and when Algy delivers the formula, our spy will attest that Brookbridge has it, and provide a sample for testing."

"And that, combined with your dictaphone recording, gets my father his money back."

"It would do," agreed Topsy, "if you hadn't retrieved the formula from Algy."

"Perhaps he hasn't noticed yet that it's missing," suggested Lady Glitz.

"Is that likely?" wondered Topsy.

"It was in a lockbox on top of the wardrobe," reflected Teddy. "Out of normal line of sight, but I did take the entire lockbox."

"Of course you did."

"I thought the necklace was in there."

"I assume you broke it open with an axe," ventured Topsy.

"Of course not." Teddy spoke with a slight sleight of professional pique. "I removed the pins from the hinges. You can't even tell it's been opened."

"Then it may not be too late," enthused Glitz. "You could put it back when he comes down for breakfast — and you could get my necklace."

"No, she can't — Algy mustn't know that he's been tricked. Teddy can only return the formula, even then that's assuming he hasn't noticed that it's missing," gloomed Topsy. "If he has then it's already too late, we're ruined."

"It's never too late, Tops." Teddy leapt from her chair. "Ring for Midgeham and tell him to come to my room with the key for Algy's." And she was gone.

It was too late.

At the very moment that Teddy was scudding down the hall to her room, Algy was already there. His plan, for he had some idea that a plan might prove necessary should he be captured by the enemy, was to claim that he had mistaken Teddy's room for the bath. Accordingly, he had taken the precaution of remaining in his pyjamas and dressing gown, and he had a towel around his neck.

The first place he looked was the top of the wardrobe. The strongbox wasn't there and so, briefly, he was stumped. He stood in the middle of the reception room and took on the dangerous and fortunately futile task of trying to think like Teddy Quillfeather. The exercise soon proved fruitless and Algy settled next on a strategy of systematic inquiry. He searched the wardrobe and writing desk and balcony and in and under Tuxedo Bird's picnic basket bed. He stared at the bookshelf in a manner designed to penetrate its secrets. He kicked listlessly at the empty wastepaper basket and checked behind a watercolour depiction of Hardy Hall commemorating a visit by William IV.

There was nothing for it. Algy put his hands on his hips and gazed at the inevitable — he was going to have to go into a lady's bedroom.

An instant later, Teddy entered the room from the hall. She left the door open for expediency, such that Midgeham need not knock, and was about to go into her bedroom wherein to change into fast and form-fitting burglar-wear, when she saw Tuxedo Bird on the balcony, somehow appearing cold and forgotten. She crossed to the balcony doors, bade the penguin enter, closed the doors, and turned to see Algy coming out of her bedroom wearing a bathing robe.

"Ah," explained Algy.

"What ho, Algo," greeted Teddy. "Get lost on the way to the bathroom?"

Simply because that had been exactly what he was going to claim, Algy felt now that the pretext was compromised. Also, he had been caught coming out of Teddy's bedroom.

"Ah, no," quickly countered Algy, thinking on his feet. "No, I came to put this note under your pillow."

To back up this ill-considered strategy, Algy withdrew from his pocket the letter he'd written to Portion. He felt instantly at ease, for he was sure that this was a winning tactic — he was, after all, at Hardy Hall that weekend with explicit instructions to romance Theodora Quillfeather. Who could possibly find anything suspicious about a handsome young man leaving a note for an attractive young lady with whom he shared the intimate proximity of a country house weekend. He smiled a sly, one-sided smile and leaned against the door jamb and swung the letter between urbane and worldly fingertips, the picture of a dauntless man with a flawless plan.

"Then why didn't you?"

"Hmm?"

"Why didn't you put the letter under my pillow?"

Teddy asked that one.

"What letter?"

That one was Portion, standing at the door.

Algy saw straight away that Portion was wearing her glasses, and in a flash he discarded the first scheme that entered his mind, that of making sounds like a penguin. Instead he quickly returned the letter to his pocket, opened his mouth, and left it that way.

"It's certainly none of my affair if you wish to leave a letter for Miss Quillfeather, Mister Brookbridge," said Portion with the warm amiability of a midnight wind sweeping across the arctic tundra.

"No," Algy managed to blurt. "No, it's…" He removed the letter from his pocket and stared at it, seeking inspiration which, in a manner of speaking, came to him. "It's not what you think…" He smiled at Teddy and then at Portion, then at the letter and then, for good measure, at Tuxedo Bird. "Not at all." He crossed the room and handed the letter to Portion. "If you'll just read it — to yourself, Miss Beanfield — you'll fully understand."

Portion read the note.

"Yes, very well," she said. "I believe this is for you, Miss Quillfeather."

"No, Portion…" Algy dispensed with the clever cloak of pretence. "As you can see, it's addressed to you."

"'My dearest darling dove,'" read Portion aloud.

"Portion, surely," corrected Algy. "My dearest darling Portion."

"Dove," Portion assured him before continuing, "*'Can't tell you how much it grieves me to have to hide like this. I adore that you came to my room last night but it's for the best that we were interrupted or I'd have soon had you in my arms and might have never let you go.'* Yes, I do apologise for the interruption, it won't happen again."

"No, Portia, the note is for you," insisted Algy with a slight screech of desperation.

"*'Always thinking of you,'*" continued Portion, "*'my statuesque bride.'*"

Portion looked a considerable distance up at Algy.

"For me, you say, Mister Brookbridge," she said in a tone like a top-quality razorblade. "Is it in some sort of code?"

"I thought you'd like that bit," whimpered Algy.

"*'PS,'*" Portion twisted the knife. "*'I shall place this under your pillow so that you'll know that I was here in your room.'*"

Portion folded the letter and handed it back to Algy.

"You needn't place this under Miss Quillfeather's pillow after all, Mister Brookbridge," pointed out Portion. "She already knows that you were in her room."

This had the air of one of the great parting lines and, accordingly, Portion departed.

"My mother said she couldn't understand why you're still available," said Teddy. "Mystery solved."

"You must explain to her." Algy handed Teddy the note.

"Explain what?" asked Teddy. "That I found you in my room and you justified it by saying that you were putting this note under my pillow?"

Algy went to the door and surveyed the hall. He closed the door but nevertheless spoke in hushed tones.

"You know perfectly well what I'm doing here, Teddy."

"You're looking for the formula for Stickle."

"I assume, since I have not yet been asked to leave the house, that you have yet to tell Lord Turville that I took it." Algy assumed his full height and majesty for an effect entirely undermined by the fact that he still spoke in whispers.

"You assume correctly." Teddy moved the conversation away from the door and towards the balcony. "What makes you think I've got it?"

"Very clearly, Teddy, that's why you were in my room yesterday," whispered Algy. "Does Lord Turville know it's gone?"

"He does," said Teddy. "But he doesn't realise that it was you who took it — he just thinks someone cleared out his safe. He suspects a drifter."

"Really?"

"That's what he said," alleged Teddy.

"And he seems so intelligent."

"Book smarts." Teddy nodded knowingly. "You want it back?"

"I must have it, Tedds." Algy spoke with rising hope and lowering tones. "Lord Turville stole it from my father."

"Did he now?"

"I know it sounds extraordinary," admitted Algy. "My father has something of a reputation for ill-treating his business partners and creditors and debtors and staff and small animals, but, really... well, in point of fact he's probably a good deal worse than most people realise, but he swears that the formula is his."

"So I take it you'd like it back."

"Yes, please." Algy nodded enthusiastically but then stopped and steadied a suspicious squint on Teddy. "Why would you just let me have it?"

"I wouldn't."

"Oh." Algy considered this, turning over persuasions and prompts in his mind until settling on "But, Tedds, I really must have it."

"You can have it back, Algy, on one condition."

"Name it."

"I want the necklace."

"What necklace?"

Teddy didn't reply to this in words. She crossed her arms before her and raised a dangerously meaningful eyebrow.

"Lady Turville's emerald catastrophe?" guessed, correctly, Algy.

"Take it or leave it." Teddy's eyebrow grew sharper, her arms crosser.

"But, why, Teddy?" Algy wondered in a whisper. "It's horrible."

"It is. It's also worth a fortune, as you well know," countered Teddy. "And I have cause to believe that my parents will soon require me to sell my car. It is my wish, should this come to pass, to be in a position to buy it."

"Right, if that's your final word." Algy shot the cuffs of his terry cloth dressing gown. "If you'll just give me the formula, I shall come by here, say, same time tomorrow morning to deliver the necklace."

"Necklace first."

"Oh, I say, Teddy, be reasonable."

"This is me being reasonable," said Teddy. "And why should I be reasonable, after the way you trifled with the affections of poor Portia."

A grimace passed over Algy's face, like that of a man with gout and a slipped disk remembering a grave loss and pulling off a hangnail.

"I say, Teddy, you couldn't take a crack at explaining things to Portia, could you?"

"After I have the necklace." Teddy held up a 'not another word' hand, for Algy appeared to have one more appeal in the chamber. In fact, he did, but it was going to be something along the lines of 'oh, do come along', and even he judged that one best saved for a more desperate moment.

"Right, well then." Algy gathered up his dignity. "I'll just bid you a jolly pip pip."

And he was off.

Algy's immediate plan was to carry on as normal, that is, to take a bath. Beyond that his mind was a blank. He was not a man who plans his actions for the same reason that he wasn't a man who dances principal roles with the Royal Ballet — he had no talent for it. He had come to Hardy House with not so much a plan as a goal — to leave with the formula for Stickle. When the opportunity presented itself he seized it — he was quite good at seizing things — and then he had the formula and, more importantly, he had the key to gaining his father's favour and blessing to marry Portia Beanfield, the only woman he ever would and ever could love.

And now he had nothing — not the formula and not Portia Beanfield, and recovering both meant providing Teddy with Lady Turville's necklace.

Which is why his mind was a blank, for when Algy had last seen the necklace it was in Lord Turville's safe.

CHAPTER NINE

Wherein Mozart's range is left largely unexplored, and Algy receives the call of the wild and he, in time, replies.

"What I don't understand…" Aunty Azalea said as she peered out the bedroom door.

"Just a moment, if you please, Aunty," interrupted Teddy. "I need a moment to say 'Augh! Where the devil did you come from?'"

"The bedroom."

"No, I know that, Aunts, what I mean is how is it that Algy didn't see you?"

"I was disguised," answered Azalea, as one stating an obvious fact.

"Disguised? In my bedroom? As what were you disguised? A bed?"

"Yes." This was said, again, as though it shouldn't have needed saying. "I sort of mingle with the bedclothes, sometimes. It's a very comfortable place to hide. Often I've fallen asleep waiting for the vicar to leave."

"This goes some distance to explaining why Algy hid the formula for Stickle practically in plain view," observed Teddy. "The man has all the imagination and guile of a newborn tulip. Now, what is it that you don't understand?"

"I was going to say, what I don't understand…"

"His Lordship asked me to bring you a key, Madame." Midgeham appeared at that moment at the still-open door, pushing a tea trolley.

"You couldn't make it coffee, could you, Midgeham?"

"This is a breakfast tray for your aunt," reported the butler.

"Oh, right, well she's..." Teddy referenced the spot where the quarry was last spotted. Azalea had disappeared. "She's coming right back, Midgers. You can leave it here."

"Very good, Madame."

"And I won't be needing that key, after all."

"Very good, Madame."

"Oh, uhm, Midgeminder?" offhanded Teddy.

"Yes, Madame?"

"Say I had something valuable that wanted safekeeping..." Teddy idly examined the tea trolley, "...what would you recommend?"

"I would take the liberty of suggesting that you raise the matter with His Lordship, Madame," said Midgeham. "He has several strongboxes on the premises."

"Such as that in which he keeps his dictaphone cylinders," suggested Teddy.

"Among others, Madame, yes."

"Excellent. And you have the combination to the dictaphone safe, have you?"

"No, Madame," differed Midgeham. "To my knowledge, only His Lordship knows the combination to any of the dozen safes and strongboxes on the premises."

"Quite sure?" To maintain the air of nonchalance about the exchange, Teddy poured a cup of tea and stirred it with a stick of toast. "He has no understudy in case he forgets a combination?"

"His Lordship very rarely forgets anything."

"No, I expect that's so."

"Even so," elaborated Midgeham, "on the one occasion that His Lordship did, in fact, misrecollect the combination to the gun cabinet — it had remained locked for many years — it proved necessary to have it opened by acetylene torch, at some considerable expense."

"I'm reassured, Midgelet," said Teddy, frankly.

"I'm most glad to have been of service, Madame. If there will be nothing else?"

"It's hard to imagine how there could be," Teddy assured him. "Unless you'd care to cavort with my penguin."

"A most generous and tempting proposition, Madame," said the butler with the grace of his vocation, "but I must supervise the footmen in the de-icing of the lower balconies and footbridge."

"Another time, then."

"Thank you, Madame."

Midgeham bowed his way out of the room and, this time, Teddy closed the door.

"What I don't understand..." Aunty Azalea said as she peered out the bedroom door, "...is what you're going to do when Mister Brookbridge gives you the necklace. He'll be expecting you to turn over the formula for Stickle."

"Then I suppose I'll just have to turn over the formula for Stickle." Teddy handed a cup of tea to Aunty Azalea. She took it to the writing desk and peered into it.

"It's got crumbs in it."

"You don't visit much, Aunty A," noted Teddy. "That's the only way it comes in country houses these days. I think Queen Mary started the fashion."

"Will Lord Turville not notice that the formula is missing?" Azalea drank her tea in the fashion of Queen Mary.

"He has done." Teddy wheeled her aunt's breakfast over to the writing table and pulled up a footstool. "He wants Algy to have it. It's all part of a complex and desperate plan to keep my father from losing the entire family fortune on a glue that dissolves aeroplanes."

"I see."

"Papa financed the development of Stickle, even and especially when costs spiralled out of control as, I understand, they tend to do in cases of unproven, untested, and non-existent technologies," explained Teddy. "This monumental blunder is mitigated, slightly, by the fact that he had a guaranteed buyer for the end product — Abernathy Brookbridge promised to make good on my father's investment in exchange for 90% of the profits."

"That was very kind of him," Azalea judged it.

"It wasn't, actually, it was an exploitative plundering of Papa's diminishing capital and credit." Teddy topped up Azalea's tea and poured a cup for herself. "And even then he had no intention of fulfilling the agreement, because the offer itself was just a pretext to provide an opportunity to steal the formula."

"Why, that's dreadful." Azalea added milk to her tea and stirred it with a stick of toast. "Something really ought to be done."

"Something was done," recounted Teddy. "Topsy set out a plan to catch Abernathy red-handed and make him pay up, but some busybody threw a wrench into it."

"I see." Azalea chewed briefly on a sip of tea.

"The plan hinges on two critical elements — the security of a certain dictaphone cylinder which, when played on a particular machine renders an unmistakable performance of a verbal contract, and Algy Brookbridge coming into possession of the formula without knowing that he's supposed to."

"Then, why didn't you just let him find it here?" wondered Azalea.

"Because I need to get Glitz's necklace back for her. Topsy used it as cover, so that Algy could steal it along with the formula and, in Algy's mind at least, sow the seeds of suspicion hither, thither, and, time permitting, yon."

"That seems very callous of Lord Turville."

Teddy raised an instructive finger. "Well, naturally, Aunts, it takes a hard, hard man to do whatever it is that he does. In any case, he thinks it's insured. And ugly. In fact, he knows it's ugly, but he doesn't know that everyone else knows it, too, or at least that's what Glitz believes."

Azalea paused and oval-eyed over her cup. "Then, Algernan Brookbridge is a jewel thief." Somehow, her eyes grew wider. "It must have been he who took Lady Woolpits' necklace during the shooting weekend at the Hollows."

"I don't think so," said Teddy. "In fact, I suspect that's why Lord Turville invited so many people who were present for the Woolpit heist — to give Algy cover. He's no jewel thief."

"But that means..."

"Yes — it means that there's still a real jewel thief here at Hardy Hall."

❦

There was little Teddy could do to advance her forces any further on the Algy front, but she still had much hot oil to pour over Bobo's battlements and Stilts continued to pose a threat from the air.

Accordingly, she dressed for guerilla socialising — a turquoise flapper wrapper with not only a low hemline but sleeves, and very serious sleeves at that. The enemy should never know exactly what to expect, though, so she added cuban heels with patent-leather straps, and took to the trenches.

Passing the library, which she regarded very much as no-man's land, Teddy detected an assault on a civilian — strains of *Eine Kleine Nachtmusik* could be heard, as could Bobo quoting *Julius Caesar,* *"Men at some time are masters of their fates. The fault, dear Brutus, is not in our stars but in ourselves..."* He completed the minuetto and added, *"Beware the ides of March."*

"That's so true," sighed the voice of Portion Beanfield.

"What ho, fellow inmates." Teddy burst into the music room, leveraging the element of surprise. The effect was complete and thorough. Portion, who had been standing at Beauregard's shoulder and turning the music sheets for him, started like a grasshopper training for the Olympics. She pulled her hand from the pages as though they had suddenly burst into flames and, in a flash, failed to convert the motion into an awkward wave.

"Good morning, Miss Quillfeather."

"Oh, Portion, do leave it out, won't you?" suggested Teddy. "Whatever you think Algy was doing in my room, he wasn't."

"I'm sure I don't know what you mean," squeaked Portion as she tottered on her heels to the door. "Good day, Miss Quillfeather, Beauregard." She made a dignified exit after fumbling only briefly with the doorknob.

"What's that you're tinkling, Bobo?" Teddy leaned on the piano. "Is that *Monkey Doodle-Do* from *Cocoanuts?*"

"Ehm…" Beauregard affected to focus on the sheet music. "Oh — *Eine Kleine Nachtmusik.*"

"Oh, that's right. I'm always confusing those two. Play something else."

"Else?"

"Different," clarified Teddy. "Something that isn't what you're playing now. This is one of the pieces that used to set off poor Grandpapa."

"Set off?"

"I mean in the psychological sense," specified Teddy. "You know, the way a red cape enrages a bull or human contact causes my Aunty Azalea to hide under a bed. Two notes of *Eine Kleine Nachtmusik* — or *Monkey Doodle-Doo,* for that matter — and Grandpapa Quillfeather would instantly start clucking like a chicken."

"Really?"

"And the extraordinary thing is, he didn't think he was a chicken," recounted Teddy. "He'd just carry on clucking about the gold standard or the national coal strike or whatever and the prime minister, bless his heart, would play right along, occasionally asking 'bok bok?'"

"Surely not."

"So you can see why Mama wants to marry me off as soon as possible," Teddy examined her fingernails casually, "before the family curse kicks in."

"I think this is all we have…" Beau sifted the sheet music before him.

"That's okay, just play something you know," urged Teddy. "I understand from the Woolpits that you were able to advise them to insure Lady Dora's necklace just in time for it to be nicked when you were on that shooting weekend with them."

Beau struggled with the barrage and eventually found himself playing *Au Claire de la Lune.*

"There was no great wisdom to it." He fumbled the left hand, which was now a full two beats behind the right. "It was simply sound advice. I'm very happy it worked out so well for them, of course, but in the end I almost wish I'd said nothing."

"Why's that, Bobo?"

"I'm afraid…" Beau broke his train of thought, briefly, to synchronise his right and left hands, which carried off on their own, repeating the first line of *Au Claire de la Lune* in a carefree, laissez-faire loop. "I'm afraid that I arranged the coverage through an insurance cooperative in which I and several friends had invested — the Woolpits' claim drove the cooperative into liquidation."

"No hard feelings?"

"How can there be?" Beau managed to liberate his right hand to play the second and third lines but his left, by all appearances, had moved on to something of its own invention. "It was my idea, after all."

"I mean, hard feelings from your friends and fellow investors."

"Few of them were in a position to notice, fewer still in a position to care."

"Kind of a coincidence, don't you find?" Teddy examined the fingernails of her other hand with equal if not greater detachment. "A robbery so soon after the Woolpit necklace is insured."

"In my line one grows accustomed to these little quirks of fortune." The effort to inject a casual tone while resynchronising his hands took its toll, and Beau was now playing *Twinkle Twinkle Little Star.*

"What line is that, exactly, Bobo?" Teddy now found cause to measure the fingernails of both hands against one another. "Concert pianist?"

"Investment counsellor." Beau's hands collided, had a mild disagreement over tempo, and went their separate ways. "I have the good fortune to have a small talent for the City markets, and the even greater fortune of many friends who trust me with their spare scraps and oddments."

"Oh, that's right, so you told me." Teddy tapped a fingernail on the piano to the tune of *Frère Jaques,* which Beau's left hand began to play. "In fact, Topsy told me that you were offering shares in Stickle to the Woolpits."

"Not me." Beau added *'Dormez-vous? Dormez-vous?'* under his breath. "They simply asked me my opinion, and I said that it was an excellent investment, a conclusion I drew from the fact that your father is so heavily invested."

"She knew that too, did she?"

"Who?"

"Lady Woolpit. Didn't you hear about Stickle from her?"

"No, I knew about it before they inquired." Beau's left hand tapped a conclusive 'din din don' and his right a trailing 'merrily merrily merrily merrily, life is but a dream.' "I learned of it from Stilts Stollery."

Algy's mind was a blank, again.

Soon after leaving Teddy he had his inspiration — she wanted the necklace, the necklace was in the safe, he knew the combination to the safe — his path was clear; he needed to open the safe and retrieve the necklace. He was — briefly, it will come to pass — elated and very slightly alarmed by his ready guile.

After a quick and comparatively cheerful bath which, it will soon be discovered, was a strategic blunder of similar proportion to invading Russia in winter, Algy climbed into winter tweeds off which he popped two buttons and, carrying his shoes for greater stealth, went to the drawing room. He knocked on Lord Turville's office door, waited, knocked again, and then went in. So far, the plan was unfurling like a whip. He approached the safe, glanced around out of shere instinct, and turned the combination.

The safe didn't open. Algy's memory is such that he was as certain that he'd dialled the correct combination as he was that his father, Portion, Teddy, and now this safe, were all giving him the short end of an already badly stunted stick. Nevertheless, he tried the combination again and, predictably, it didn't work for a second time.

And so Algy's mind, as was previously touched upon, was a blank. He decided, after staring at the safe for some two minutes, to get breakfast.

❦

"Why are you carrying your shoes, Algernon?" asked Glitz when Algy entered the second dining room.

He looked at his shoes. They were, indeed, in his hand.

"I..." Algy searched his mind for an explanation but, as mentioned, it was a blank. "I was taking a bath."

Country house rules applied, of course, and so this reasoning was accepted by Lord and Lady Turville, who remained the only other occupants of the breakfast room. That had only become true again some five minutes earlier, when Lord Turville returned from his office, where he had changed the combination of his safe while, erring in idle self-indulgence, Algy was having a bath.

Algy put his shoes on and briefly considered pretending that he had come to the breakfast room for that expressed purpose, and then leaving. He wanted breakfast, but he wanted to avoid an awkward encounter with Lord and Lady Turville even more. His plan — less a plan, as such, than it was a jittery instinct — had been to rely heavily on the practice of stout denial. Of course he didn't take the formula for Stickle. What is Stickle, even? I don't easily take offence, Your Lordship, but I daresay this accusation is a rather novel construction to put on your duties as host.

Lord Turville's ambitions for the encounter, as it happened, aligned perfectly with those of Algy. Ideally, Algy would have taken the formula and enjoyed the rest of his weekend at Hardy Hall without ever actually encountering Lord Turville. It's a big place, Hardy Hall, and it's not entirely impossible to go days without engaging with anyone who's broken into your safe in the dead of night. Failing that — and that had most definitely failed thanks to the intervention of Teddy Quillfeather — Algy would be put at his ease, never suspecting that he had fallen into a cleverly laid trap.

Casual diversion was to Lord Turville what stout denial was intended to be for Algy, and so he said, "Strangest thing — Lady Gladys' necklace has been stolen from my safe."

"What necklace?" replied Algy, quick as a cat. "What's a necklace? I mean to say, which necklace is that?"

"Green emerald thing," explained Topsy. "Doubtless you won't recall it, but Gladdy was quite attached to it, weren't you, dear?"

Glitz looked up from her toast, at which she had been staring in the hope that staring at toast turned one invisible. "I designed it myself."

"Not really." Algy spoke, once again, from raw reflex. "I mean to say, oh, really?"

"Nothing to concern yourself with, of course," offhanded Topsy. "It's insured. I mention it more as a matter of interest."

Lord Turville's intention had been to put Algy's mind to rest, giving the impression that all attention was on this missing necklace and so the theft of the formula had passed unnoticed. The strategy was founded on the assumption that Teddy had managed to return the formula to Algy's room before he noticed that it was missing, or that she was in that very moment doing so.

Algy's mind was not at rest. Certainly, it was no longer a blank, but it was definitely not at rest. He hadn't known how he was going to extract the necklace from the safe but he had, until a moment ago, at least known where it was. Now, the chain of dependencies that would lead to his reconciliation and eventual marriage had just grown longer by two sturdy links. Before even beginning to work out how to retrieve the necklace, he had to work out where it was, and that in turn depended on figuring out who took it.

"Any idea who took it?" asked Algy, very much playing the long odds.

"None at all," Topsy was quick to assure him. "Probably a drifter."

Algy groaned but managed to change it, to the ears of a charitable audience, into a 'hmmm' of indecision.

"Urrrmmmm… Eggs or toast. Why not both."

To his almost audible relief, Lord and Lady Turville at that moment excused themselves to carry on about their post-breakfast day. Topsy had letters to dictate and Glitz urgently needed to go to her room and tremble under dim lighting.

Algy sat at a chair nearest the window and ate his egg and toast — which might as well have been paper and paste for all the attention he was giving it — and he stared at the grounds of Hardy Holm. No new snow had fallen but none had melted, either, and this stalemate kept the entirety of Kent, right up to the moat, an unbroken roll of shimmery, silvery plain and vale. As Algy gazed his gloom upon the grounds, Tuxedo Bird teetered past his line of vision, tracing the outer edge of the moat with waddly little footprints in the snow.

And Algy had his first really useful inspiration.

❦

Lord Turville was pleased with his performance. Everything, he felt sure, was as it should be. Algy had the formula and he — Topsy — had seized an opportunity to reassure Algy that he was under no suspicion. As a bonus, he'd ridded the household of that hideous necklace.

He organised his correspondence on his desk in order of; to be read, already read, to be read a second time, and to be answered. He opened the cabinet with the lockbox of dictaphone cylinders, opened the lockbox, and retrieved a blank and noted, as a passing point of peace of mind, that the recording of the verbal contract was safely where it belonged. He closed the safe and locked it and turned the dial twenty-three clicks.

He brought the fresh cylinder to his desk so that he might fit it into the machine but decided, on balance, that it would be better to stare with unbelieving eyes — the dictaphone was gone.

CHAPTER TEN

*In which the many accomplishments of Emily Dickenson are studied,
as are the hidebound attitudes of London's West End.*

*"It Ruffles Wrists of Posts
As Ankles of a Queen
Then stills its Artisans — like Ghosts
Denying they have been,"*

mused Stilts, as he stood at the library window, his back strategically angled to the door. He turned as Teddy entered. "Oh, what ho, Tedds."

"Emily Dickenson," identified Teddy.

"Yes, I believe so." Stilts glanced discreetly down at a handful of notes. "I often think of it when I consider the snow," still with an eye on his notes, "and the way it sifts from leaden sieves, and powders all the wode, fills with alabaster wool the wrinkles of the road, and whatnot."

"Very impressive, Stilts," lauded Teddy. "It's wood, though, not wode."

"But then it doesn't rhyme with road."

"Emily was a rebel," sympathised Teddy. "She was the first woman to fly solo across the continental United States, you know."

"Of course I know that."

"Of course," Teddy acknowledged. "Midgeham said you hoped I'd come and see you."

"Did he?" puzzled Stilts. "Oh, right, yes, I mentioned to him that, you know, should he happen to see you, it would be perfectly fine with me if he told you that I was in the library, as it were."

By yet another extraordinary confluence of cases, Midgeham entered the library at that moment, pushing a trolley of tea for two.

"Your tea, Mister Stollery."

"What a happy coincidence," Stilts declared it. "Thank you, Midgeham."

Midgeham silently slipped away and Stilts splashed about with the pottery and silverware until some residual tea was in two cups, and then he returned to his vigil by the window. He sipped his tea and then repressed a small laugh, as though recalling a witticism learnt an age ago.

"I believe it was Byron who said, *'The English Winter, ending in July, to recommence in August...'*"

"It was," confirmed Teddy, who took her tea to the divan at the other window, so that they were both inspired by the winter scene. "It's *from Don Juan.*"

"Yes, that sounds right."

"Do very kindly leave it out, Stilts."

"I'm not sure I know what you mean."

"Name a poem by Byron."

"Oh, well, let us see... there are so very many to choose from..." Stilts rubbed his chin reflectively, causing the entire structure to sway and some tea to leap from his cup to his saucer. *"Don Juan* comes to mind."

"And who was riding the winner of last year's London Cup at Ally Pally?"

"Todd 'Tadpole' Emmerson on Halalie. Finished at seven to one after trailing second-place finisher Salisbury Sue, ridden by local legend Specks Spelter in his first race after serving three months at Dartmoor on a charge of impersonating a child for personal gain," recalled Stilts with ease. "And it was his birthday. And a sticky track."

"Talking of sticky tracks, Stilton old cheese," veered Teddy, "do I understand that you tried to invest in Stickle?"

"Ehm, yes, I believe I did." Stilts spoke distractedly as he endeavoured to sort his notes without looking at them.

"How did you even hear about it, anyway? Wasn't it meant to be top secret?"

"Oh, absolutely…" Stilts side-eyed Teddy as she gazed out the window. "Yes. A secret… Very much a… yes, here we go." He sipped his tea as though he'd been sipping tea all his life. "Rather puts me in mind of Christina Rossetti's little number, 'Winter: My Secret'…

'I tell my secret?
No indeed, not I:
Perhaps some day, who knows?
But not today; it froze, and blows, and snows,
And you're too curious: fie!'

…and so on in that vein."

Teddy regarded Stilts beneath a hooded brow.

"How did you hear about it?"

"Oh, I couldn't possibly say, Tedds," blaséd Stilts. "I read rather a lot of poetry, and whatnot. You'd be quite surprised, I expect."

"I daresay I would," agreed Teddy. "I meant, who told you about Stickle?"

"Oh, right. Stickle." Stilts mentally reviewed his notes. He had perforce limited himself to the theme of winter and so Stickle, particularly on such short notice, offered no obvious segué to Victorian poetry. "Major Lonegrave."

"How did he hear about it?"

"I assumed Lady Woolpit," said Stilts.

"Stands to reason." Teddy made a show of finishing her tea. "I thought you restricted your financial interests to precious stones, their treatment in illness and in health."

"In all candour, Teddy, that's what I told Beauregard Pilewright." Stilts collected Teddy's cup and geared up for another assault upon the teapot. "He and I make a poor financial syndicate."

"Did he by any chance get you to invest in an insurance cooperative?"

"Certainly not, Teddy." The offence caused Stilts to drop a spoonful of sugar into the creamer, and then stir it. "I hope you credit me with more intelligence than that. No, Pilewright talked me into investing in a musical comedy."

"Oh, right, that's much more sensible."

"Would have been quite jolly, though, wouldn't it?" Stilts poured the tea, as he does ineluctably everything else, from a height. "Having our own musical comedy, I mean to say."

"Our?"

"Well, I know that you like that sort of thing — theatre and poetry and whatnot." Stilts handed over Teddy's tea. "It had real horses on stage, and a smashing choral number to close out the second act with a can-can line roller skating into a swimming pool."

"Let me guess," guessed Teddy, "no London theatre would take it on."

"You could have knocked me over with a feather." Stilts shook his head in slow wonder. "Not a one. Who could have predicted such a thing? Not even the Criterion, and not even after we proposed live dolphins in the pool. If anything, that made them even less interested and, I don't think I'm being overly sensitive, a bit rude."

"I thought Bobo had some rare talent for all the financial fuss," said Teddy.

"He does." Stilts grimaced at the snow, wherein he saw bitter recrimination. "I think he saves his riskiest investments for his friends, because he knows we'll forgive him."

"But you haven't forgiven him," pointed out Teddy.

"I'm nobody's fool, either," said Stilts with cool pride. "After the catastrophes that were *First Past the Pond* and The Thames Riverboat Casino…"

"Is that what it sounds like?"

"Probably," said Stilts. "How could we possibly have known that it was illegal?"

"I think it's widely understood."

"And so, fool me twice, shame on you…"

"That's not how that goes, Stilts."

"It well ought to be. In any case, that's why I no longer invest with Pilewright. We're an unlucky combination." Stilts swirled his tea like a man who's never swirled nor seen anything swirl in his life. "Rather like the last line of Shelley's little arrangement, don't you think? Ode to the West Wind. I believe it goes something like *'The trumpet of a prophecy! O Wind, if winter comes, can spring be far behind?'*"

"That puts you in mind of investing with Bobo."

"A bit, yes," persisted Stilts. "Something about the patina, I think. Similar, don't you find?"

"To me it recalls *'As if his whole vocation was endless imitation','*" recited Teddy.

"Byron?"

"Wordsworth," corrected Teddy. "It's from *Stilts Stollery Ought to Stick to Handicapping Horses*. Wasn't there a very winny three-year-old called Lord Byron?"

"You're thinking of Lord By-A-Nose," enthused Stilts. "A very promising colt. Had a disappointing Epsom but went on to sire no less than three Derby placers and pull Queen Mary's coach when she arrived in Bognor Regis to dry out for three weeks."

"That's more like it."

"And, young Theodora, if you can keep it to yourself, I'm in a position to put you onto well cited and supported scuttle that Lord

By-A-Nose has a grandson receiving very long odds in the third next Saturday at Plumpton."

"Welcome back, Stilts."

"It's just, well, dash it, Teddy," Stilts waved his cup in a wide and rueful arc, shifting the last of his tea into the saucer, "the weekend's almost over and I know how I compare standing next to a chap like Algy Brookbridge."

"You're not concerned about Algy Brookbridge, surely," marvelled Teddy. "I assure you, Stilts, that Algy has just as much chance as you have of winning my hand this weekend."

"You mean that?"

"With my heart and soul," swore Teddy. "Although, you know, he did come to my room this morning."

"Did he now?"

"With a note," recounted Teddy, as though just then remembering the details. "He meant to put it under my pillow, he said."

"Under your pillow, you say."

"Portion interrupted us." Teddy furrowed a curious brow against the gravity of the situation.

"If I might take the liberty of asking, what did Portion interrupt?"

"Us."

"And, once again, if it's not too much of a liberty, as it were, what was it that you and Mister Brookbridge were discussing?"

"Oh, you know, doves, love, industrial adhesives. That sort of thing." Teddy swirled her tea like an Olympian tea-swirler.

"Adhesives?" queried Stilts. "That comes up rather a lot in conversation with you, Teddy."

"It's a family preoccupation. My father is very interested in Stickle, and I'm very interested in my father," explained Teddy. "My mother — who is married to my father, as a bit of background — has made it clear that unless I select for her a viable son-in-law this weekend, I can wave a teary farewell to my flat in Chelsea and my car."

"They'll make you give up your flat in Chelsea?"

"And my car," repeated Teddy. "You're a bloke and couldn't possibly understand the deep emotional attachment a girl has to her motor. Imagine a bird negotiating the disposition of her wings. I was seeking leverage."

"Algy Brookbridge is leverage?" asked Stilts.

By what appeared but absolutely was not coincidence, at that moment the rugby fly half under appraisal crossed their field of vision. Algy was walking along the edge of the moat, eyes down, by all appearances tracking Tuxedo Bird by his footprints in the snow.

"What is he doing?" wondered Stilts.

"Composing another note, I shouldn't wonder." Teddy nodded at her own deft supposition. "He's a very deep thinker."

❦

Algy was thinking deep thoughts as he shuffled through the otherwise undisturbed snow.

His current thoughts had been given flight by something Lord Turville had said, specifically his allegations — sadly typical of men of his class — against a blameless drifter. The accusation had initially disheartened Algy because he had until then assumed that, wherever it might be, the necklace was at least still on the premises. But then he recalled that there had been a heavy snowfall on the night that he took the Stickle formula when — and this is key — he saw the necklace in the safe. This meant that the robbery had occurred since then, unlike further snowfall, which had not. Combining these two concrete clues into a plan of action was for Algy but the work of minutes and now he was on the grounds, looking for and, significantly, failing to find any tracks leading to or from Hardy Hall. The hall is surrounded by a moat and for all their apparent skills with breaking and entering and opening locked safes, drifters, Algy felt comfortably sure, could not fly. The necklace was still somewhere inside the house.

This realisation caused another important clue to materialise — of everyone present at Hardy Hall this weekend only five of them had also been at the Woolpit's shooting lodge when Lady Dora's necklace was stolen. He knew he hadn't done it and obviously the Woolpits hadn't stolen their own property, and so the thief had to be either Beauregard Pilewright or Major Stanley Lonegrave. On further examination of the evidence, Algy discovered that he didn't like Beauregard Pilewright. Practically an open-and-shut case.

Algy hurried back to the bridge, to the courtyard, and into the house by the main entrance where he encountered Midgeham whose expertise, he perceived in the instant, he required.

"Ah, Midgeham, my good man," he debonaired. "Can you direct me to..." and here he stopped himself. He very much needed to know which room was that of Beaureagard Pilewright, but no one must know what he'd worked out by Sherlockian logic and Brookbridgeian legwork. Algy had to recover the necklace alone and, equally importantly, anonymously.

"Certainly, sir," prompted Midgeham, who had been waiting. "To where might I direct you?"

"Can you direct me..." Algy's mind raced. "Can you direct me to my room?"

"Your room, sir?"

"I've forgotten which it is," claimed Algy, he suddenly realised, credibly. "I was moved last night, as you know. I believe I'm right next to Mister Pilewright, if that helps."

"No, sir, Mister Pilewright is in the east hall," corrected Midgeham. "You are directly opposite — the last door of the west hall, first floor."

"Oh, yes, of course." Algy affected an unconvincing and unnecessary laugh. "Because Mister Pilewright is the last door of the east hall, first floor."

"Yes, sir."

"That must be why I thought I was right next to him," suggested Algy.

"As you say, sir."

"You don't know where Mister Pilewright is at the moment, do you, Midgeham?" asked Algy in a casual manner, as though Beau's current anchorage was for him a matter of barely passing interest.

"Mister Pilewright is in the second dining room, sir, where breakfast is currently served," replied Midgeham.

"Oh, yes? Well, good for him," said Algy. "Well, good night, Midgeham."

"Good morning, sir."

Buoyed by this smooth success, Algy ambled down the main hall with an easy air, as though accompanied by something for the flute.

Fortune followed fortune as Algy found the last door of the east hall, first floor, unlocked. Fortune faltered fleetingly when Algy looked around the ensuite room of Beauregard Pilewright who travelled with no fewer than three steamer trunks.

It turned out, though, that searching three steamer trunks, four hat boxes, a boot box, and a brass and leather grooming kit can be done quite snippily when they're all impeccably organised. Algy was briefly delayed by a non-intuitive spring-guided tie-folder, and momentarily distracted and excited by what turned out to be an elaborate tie-pin rack, but within minutes he had determined that the necklace was not in the ensuite. That left the bedroom.

The first thing that Algy noticed was retroactively consequential — the bed was unmade. This was in perfect accordance with the room service schedule at Hardy Hall but it served to cast Algy's mind back to his search of Teddy's room. The bed had been unmade there, too, and it was only in that moment that he saw his mistake — somehow he had failed to look under the bed. Obviously, the strongbox containing the formula was still under Teddy's bed.

So once again Algy's mind was a turmoil and he instantly determined to, this time, avoid taking a bath before acting. He would finish searching Beau's room and, should he find the necklace, so much the better, but then he would return to Teddy's room and fetch that formula.

Empty-handed, he quit the bedroom and came face--to-face with Beauregard Pilewright.

"Oh, I say…" said Beau but then, putting the lie to it, he said nothing.

So sharpened had Algy's mind been against a coarse-grained whetstone of a morning, he didn't skip a beat before replying, "Why, Pilewright — what are you doing here?"

Algy's tone was commanding and for just an instant Beau wondered what, indeed, he was doing there.

"This is my room."

"No it isn't."

"Those are my steamer trunks," Beau offered in evidence.

"Oh, I say, I am sorry old man," capitulated Algy. "I thought this was Miss Quillfeather's room."

"Not for me to say in someone else's household, Brookbridge," Beau drew himself up and cocked a cocky eyebrow, "but I'm not sure that's not worse."

"I was leaving her a note," said Algy with cool composure. "I was just leaving it beneath her pillow, or, rather, your pillow."

"Doubtless you'll want to retrieve it, then," suggested Beau.

"Hmm?"

"You'll want it back, I expect," clarified Beau. "Unless you expect me to give it to her."

"Oh, ah, no…" groped Algy. "It's not there."

"Where is it?"

"I haven't written it yet." Algy felt his cool slipping away while Beau could actually see it slipping away.

And that's how Algy Brookbridge, not ten minutes later, had come to agree to provide the lion's share of the capital that Beauregard Pilewright assured him was necessary to finance a US tour of the Elgin Marbles.

A price worth paying, reasoned Algy, and easily afforded once he'd recovered the Stickle formula and handed it over to his father. Besides which, Beau was quite convinced and convincing that the return would be, at a comfortable minimum, five times the initial investment. Probably closer to ten.

In the meantime, though, Algy was free to circumvent Teddy's demand that he steal Lady Gladys' necklace. He encountered no one as he padded down the stairs and along the north hall to Teddy's room. He once again employed the ruse of knocking first but this time took the precaution of impersonating the knock of a parlour maid. He slipped into Teddy's room.

Algy being Algy, he was surprised to discover that there was nothing under the bed. He surveyed the bedroom from where he stood. The bed had since been made but otherwise nothing obvious had changed and no new hiding places presented themselves.

With leaden heart and steps, Algy removed himself from the room. As he passed through the ensuite reception, his attention was drawn by Tuxedo Bird, who was honking noncommittaly, as though extending Algy the courtesy of acknowledgement without any real desire to engage.

Leaving a room into which one has sneaked is appreciably less trying on the spirit than sneaking into a room. Algy left his anxieties behind as he closed Teddy's door, well short of whistling a happy tune but certainly measurably lighter of heart. His guard was down, accordingly, and even when Algy's guard was up and keen, such as on the rugby field, he relied much more heavily on his ability to rise again then he did his resistance to getting knocked down in the first place. And so accordingly and unknown to him, Algy was seen by no less than two interested parties.

❦

"You should lock your door." Aunty Azalea let herself into Teddy's room some forty-five minutes after Algy had left it.

"Most people knock," Teddy reminded her.

"I can't bear loud noises, Teddy." Azalea spoke in hushed urgency, as though advising on the secret health benefits to be gained from a low tolerance for noise. "It wasn't locked this morning, either."

"I know it wasn't locked, Aunty." Teddy, who had been lying on the divan, continued to do so. "I left it open for you. Did you manage to shift the formula?"

"It's in the penguin's bed." Azalea whispered and pointed discreetly with just her eyes at Tuxedo Bird's picnic basket bed.

"That is satisfactory — Algy's already looked there and everywhere else in this room, so he won't think to do so again." Doubtless Teddy would have spoken with fewer Napoleonic airs had she known that Algy had done just that.

"I cannot put words to how anxious I was while the formula was in my room."

"More so than usual?" doubted Teddy.

"Fractionally," confessed Azalea. "But it matters to me."

"All over now, Aunts, but for wasting champagne in the winner's circle."

"You're quite certain that Algernon Brookbridge has Gladys' necklace," wondered Azalea.

129

"Well, of course he has it," said Teddy. "Who else?"

"No one I can think of. It just strikes me as odd that he hasn't yet given it to you."

"I expect he's hesitating," speculated Teddy. "The formula wins him his father's approval, but if he keeps the necklace, maybe he doesn't need his father's approval. Beneath that doughy, dopy exterior, Aunty A, beats the cold steel heart of a calculating opportunist."

"Really?"

"No, not really. He probably forgot where he put it." Teddy's attention was drawn to the door where Tuxedo Bird had appeared or, judging by his demeanour of quiet martyrdom, he'd been waiting for a while. "That's peculiar. Did you put the penguin out?"

"I can't bear to," said Azalea. "He always looks at me like he wants me to come along, but I can't swim and it breaks my heart to disappoint him."

Teddy rolled from the divan and opened the balcony doors. Tuxedo Bird waddled in with a civil nod and dropped like a felled tree into his picnic basket bed. The sound of a penguin tipping into knitting is not very distinct from that of many other flightless birds falling into all manner of woven fabrics, but Teddy knew the sound of a penguin falling onto a metal strongbox, and this most certainly was not it. She bent and frisked the picnic basket bed.

"You're quite certain you put the formula in Tuxedo Bird's bed," she asked.

"Oh, dear."

"Because it's not here now."

CHAPTER ELEVEN

In which Algy receives instruction on phrases, hardware, and headgear of use to the adventurous traveller to the Indian subcontinent.

"Of course Algy has the formula. I let him think that he stole it from my room."

Teddy made this false claim with the calm composure of the club and international class fibber that she was.

"Well, this is no good, Teddy." Lord Turville said this with only a shade of an idea how right he was. He'd sent for Teddy the moment he'd noticed his dictaphone missing, but it had taken her until nearly lunchtime to free her schedule, and in that time he'd worked up an ostentatiously grim view of affairs that still, nevertheless, fell short of the truth.

"It's all psychology, Topsy." Teddy opened the office door, verified that the drawing room was clear of spies, and closed the door again so that they were safely alone in Lord Turville's office. "I couldn't just give it to him."

"You have to get it back."

"Get it back?" ghasted Teddy. "After all the lures and leads I carefully laid to get it to him?"

"Either that or the dictaphone," compromised His Lordship. "He can't have both."

"That does seem a trifle gluttonous, doesn't it?" agreed Teddy. "Has he got both?"

"Who else would have taken it?"

"I might have," speculated Teddy. "Have you any idea how much fun I could have with a dictaphone?"

"Did you?"

"No." Teddy dropped into a deep leather visitor's chair. "I've been far too busy."

Lord Turville tamped the bowl of his pipe like a man with a strong antipathy to tobacco.

"Are you allowed to ignite that indoors?" asked Teddy.

"Gladdy makes exceptions on special occasions." Topsy struck a match and puffed his pipe into a crackling conflagration. "Such as when we're about to be financially ruined."

"Can't you just get another dictaphone?" asked Teddy, reasonably.

"Not like this one." Topsy shook his head slowly and sadly at the spot where this one used to happily perch on the edge of his desk. "Everyone recorded on it sounds like an auctioneer on any other machine. On that machine it's a living reproduction — you can hear your father winding his watch — the recording of Abernathy Brookbridge agreeing to compensate your father and myself for our investment is only evidence on the machine that Algy's taken."

"I see."

"Do you, Teddy?" interrogated Topsy in a rushed hush. "There's something I haven't mentioned, because I didn't want you to worry unduly — your father and I didn't just invest in Stickle, we've borrowed heavily, and the first repayment comes due very, very soon."

"How soon?"

"Last Wednesday."

"Blimey," expelled Teddy. "Good thing you didn't mention it."

"I believe that any worrying done now would not be done unduly," judged Topsy. "Your father and I are bankrupt unless we get that dictaphone back from Algy."

"Well, we're not going to."

"Why not?"

"Because Algy doesn't need it," replied Teddy. "He only needs you to not have it, so immediately after he took it he'd have thrown it into the moat."

Lord Turville groaned and looked forlornly at the empty dictaphone dock.

"Furthermore," piled on Teddy. "Algy didn't take it."

"Why do you say that?"

"Because he doesn't know about the verbal agreement," said Teddy. "So he has no reason to take your dictaphone, and if Algy were to have taken it he'd have done so at the same time he took the formula and the necklace, not a full day later in broad daylight."

"I say, that's true," realised Topsy.

"Algy's an opportunistic thief," said Teddy with light disdain. "Barely even a thief at all, by any professional standard."

❧

"I'm far from a professional thief myself, you understand, but you're what we'd have called, back in Jaipur, a *badirchand.*"

Major Lonegrave saw fit to give this lesson in Raj linguistics upon returning from the games room, where he'd sustained a minor darts injury, and finding Algy in his room.

"I'm afraid that you have me at a disadvantage." Algy was at his wits' end and his mind, not unusually, was a blank, but he knew an insult when he heard one.

"Difficult to translate from the original Hindi." The major put a hand to his chin and stared into the colonial past. "Oh, in fact, no it isn't. Means 'dolt'. Almost a direct translation, now I think of it."

It was a fair comment, given the circumstances, which positioned the major at his bedroom door watching Algy struggle to free himself of the bed, under which he had crawled when he heard the ensuite door open. He'd been searching Major Lonegrave's room and, owing to the irresistible hold they exercise over all young men, he was wearing a pith helmet.

"I am not accustomed to being accused of being a thief, Major." Algy spoke as cooly as could be expected of a man stuck under a bed.

"What about a dolt?" inquired the major with a clinical curiosity. "I expect you're quite habituated."

Algy tried to form an explanation from the facts to hand, like a chef improvising a dish from a box of icing sugar and some beans. He'd discarded immediately the pretext he'd employed with Beau — claiming that he thought he was in Teddy's room — because, partially, it had failed once already, but mainly because Major Lonegrave's room was a clutter of safari suits and boots, a long-barrelled hunting rifle, and, most significantly and undeniably, a pith helmet. Furthermore, he hadn't had the chance to search properly, having started this time with the bedroom reasoning, erroneously, that it would be quicker.

"I'll tell you the truth, Major." Algy assumed that grave, we-both-men-of-the-world demeanour that's so notoriously difficult to bring off stuck under a bed. "I'll ask you to keep it between us, for the moment, but there is a thief on the premises."

"I know there is. I just caught him in my bedroom."

"I meant, Major, another thief," confided Algy. "I mean to say, not me. Someone has taken Lady Turville's necklace."

"The Spirit of Myawaddy?"

"No. I'm referring to Lady Turville's emerald necklace." Algy finally removed the pith helmet which, he felt, was impeding his escape efforts. "You can't have missed it. Looks like a stained glass flamingo."

"That's The Spirit of Myawaddy," explained the Major. "It's been stolen?"

"Right out of His Lordship's safe," confirmed Algy. "He asked me to discreetly recover it."

"Discreetly, you say." Major Lonegrave watched Algy lift the bed fully off all four legs as he worked his way free of the scrum.

"Well, he could hardly go about searching his guests rooms himself, could he?" Algy pulled his legs from beneath the bed and saw, with a sigh, that he'd lost a shoe.

"Don't see why not?" differed the major. "Once in Nagpur, while I was a guest of Maharaja Pawar Patil, one of his wives went missing. Turned us all out of our rooms at four in the morning. And made us unlock our steamer trunks."

"I don't know that it's quite the same thing, Major."

"Turned out he'd just lost count," continued Lonegrave. "Lady Gladys hasn't lost count, has she? She has rather a lot of jewellery."

"This piece is quite special to her, Major," recalled Algy with a shudder. "She designed it herself."

"Yes…" The major shook his head in wonder. "I know."

"If I could just make use of your stick for a moment, Major." Algy, on all fours, was peering under the bed at his shoe.

"It's a whangee," corrected the major, for he felt that precision was vital in these matters.

"You won't object to me taking a bit of a look about, Major?" The shoe evaded the whangee and so Algy lifted the bed like the back end of an Austin Seven and affected a sweeping conversion.

"Not at all." Lonegrave retreated to the ensuite reception room where, in keeping with domestic customs from Kent to Nagpur, he unlocked his steamer trunk. "You won't find it here, of course, but I can tell you where you will find it."

"I say, really?" marvelled Algy. "You know who's taken the necklace?"

"No, I don't, but you'll be able to identify him easily — the Spirit of Myawaddy brings consistent ill fortune to anyone who steals it."

"Don't you have consistently ill fortune, Major?" Algy set about systematically searching the steamer trunk, which was effectively a travelling wardrobe of waterproof evening wear, river boots and sandals and all manner of footwear unsuitable to a weekend in Kent, and a bivouac tent.

"Nothing like before I sold The Spirit of Myawaddy to Lady Turville." Lonegrave opened for inspection a hatbox containing a plumed slouch-brim and a desert beret. "Time was I couldn't cross a border without some functionary charging me with smuggling some obscure thing or another. Got so bad I had to give up smuggling."

"Probably a coincidence."

"Had appalling luck at the casino," lamented the major. "Found a roulette wheel with a pronounced prejudice for twenty-nine, black."

"Surely that's a good thing, Major." Algy was standing on a chair and giving the top of the wardrobe the all-clear.

"It was my casino." Lonegrave said this with a bewildered calm, as though yet unable to fully believe the litany of vengeances visited upon him by the Spirit of Myawaddy. "Lost money every night for months before I caught on, and then the floor manager made off with all the cash in the safe."

"The safe?" queried Algy. "Did you give this floor manager the combination to the safe?"

"Well, if a man can't trust his own brother..." pronounced Lonegrave with old-school affront. "It took a lot of character for him to leave a note telling me about his affair with my wife before they ran off."

Algy stood in the middle of the room, hands on hips, surveying the field of play and pronouncing it a draw.

"But your luck has since improved, you say."

"Could hardly have got worse."

"You don't miss smuggling and gambling and thieving and the like?" asked Algy, because he was a courteous conversationalist.

"I miss the wife, a bit." The major nodded vague agreement. "She always knew just what to do whenever I was stung by a scorpion or stepped in a bear trap."

"Well, the necklace isn't here," concluded Algy as he pushed the divan back to the wall.

"I know it isn't." The major spoke with the puzzled patience of an old colonial hand obliged to repeat the obvious. "I don't even like being in the same house with the diabolical thing."

"Then, if I might ask, Major, why are you?"

"Stickle."

Algy was like Lord Turville in that he, too, had believed Stickle to be a well-guarded secret, at a degree of confidentiality somewhere between the king's exact location in time of war and the queen's whisky budget.

"Stickle, Major?" Algy spoke with what he thought was a deft indifference, but in fact sounded more like he'd been stabbed with a hat pin.

"Meant to be a revolutionary abrasive."

"You don't mean adhesive," checked Algy.

"Abrasive," confirmed Lonegrave. "Supposed to be capable of giving a glass finish to a cobblestone road."

"Have you a cobblestone road requiring a glass finish, Major?" wondered Algy honestly.

"Of course not, you young *badirchand,*" admonished the major. "Wanted to buy into Stickle. Now I've broken the curse of The Spirit of Myawady, I can afford to extend myself a bit. Invest a little money, play a bit of roulette, occasionally. Maybe take a walk outside without a pith helmet."

"You're not saying that Lord Turville sold you shares in Stickle."

"Turned me down like goose lining," recalled the major. "Denied there was any such thing as Stickle, in fact."

"Are you quite sure that there is?" asked Algy, cannily.

137

"Of course I am. Got it from an unimpeachable source. Sir Oswald and Lady Woolpit."

❦

"What ho, Portion."

Teddy found Portion where she'd been hiding, on a rustic bench between two shrubs at what would be the back of Hardy Hall if Hardy Hall had, in any practical sense, a front. The bench was on the island side of the moat opposite from the bridge and so it felt isolated and broody and an excellent location in which to be miserable. The scene was made perfect by light but ice-cold rain.

"Good afternoon, Miss Quillfeather." Portion was sitting on the bench and the bench was covered with sloppy snow and Portion didn't care. She made a little snowball of material to hand and threw it into the moat.

"Call me Penny." Teddy drew up to the bench but didn't sit. She had only added a blue, double-breasted swing coat, a feather boa and a pair of the gardener's Wellies to her inside outfit, and she didn't like sitting in wet snow.

"But, Penny's not your name," pointed out Portion.

"Neither is Miss Quillfeather, to you." Teddy watched Portion withdraw a sheet of paper from the folds of her coat and begin folding it like origami. "What are you doing, Ports?"

"Nothing of any consequence," whimsied Portion, who was wearing spectacles and flat-soled shoes. "Just amusing myself until it's time to return to London."

"Why out here in the cold?"

"I wished to remain undisturbed and out of sight," replied Portion coolly. "Might I ask how you knew to look for me here?"

138

"That's my window right there." Teddy nodded across the moat to a balcony on which Tuxedo Bird stood, flapping happily until he tripped off the balustrade into the water.

"I see, now." Portion set aside her origami and withdrew another sheet of paper. "I didn't recognise it at first without Algernon Brookbridge lingering in your room, putting notes under your pillow."

"It was just the one," offered Teddy. "Surely a chap's allowed to put one, single love letter under the pillow of a comparative stranger without developing a reputation for the practice. Algy is so much more than that. Rugby, or something, I think."

"Just the one, was it?" sniffed Portion adding, very quietly but meaningfully, "Ha."

"I know of only one."

"He put the other somewhere else," said Portion. "Doubtless in a volume of poetry, or in a drawer with your other intimate things."

"You didn't check?"

"I don't know what you mean," claimed Portion with the forced pique of the inept liar.

"You left an empty sardine tin in Tuxedo Bird's bed."

Portion folded another paper form in her lap. This one appeared to meet some sort of threshold, and so she stood and carried a little flotilla of paper boats to the moat, where she released them. Then she returned to the bench, made a tiny snowball, and launched it at the armada.

"Algy's letters?" supposed Teddy.

"Just some scrap paper for which I no longer have any use." Portion fired another missile for a direct hit, taking what looked like a sonnet to a watery grave.

"Why do you think Algy left me a second letter, Portion," asked Teddy.

"I saw him leaving your room."

139

"Ah."

"Yes. This was my thought too, exactly," said Portion. "Ah."

"Was he carrying anything?"

"Yes." Portion pistoned a snowball with the force of a cannon, scattering a squadron of couplets decorated with hearts. "He had about him an air of duplicitousness."

"Anything more substantial than that?" asked Teddy. "Something in a grey metal, perhaps?"

"Not that I noticed."

"Then when you searched my room did you happen to see such a thing?"

"Yes." Portion stooped to scrape together new and unprecedented supplies of snow. "It was in Tuxedo Bird's bed."

"Did you look inside?"

"It was locked. Why? Was it full of love letters?"

"The hinge pins had been removed," said Teddy. "You didn't open it, then. Why did you take it?"

Portion patted together a snowball the size of a cannonball. "Of course I didn't take your ridiculous steel box. What possible interest might I have in Algnernon Brookbridge's love letters?"

And with that, Portion stood and heaved her snowcannonball into the moat, where it burst the surface in a great spout and splash, and then sank, drawing with it most of the fleet before returning to the surface, alone. She stood on the shore and observed the carnage with the cold detachment of the career admiral.

Teddy joined her on the banks and watched a rag-tag unit formed of a postcard, an envelope, and a ribbon make a break for open seas.

"If you didn't take it, then who did?"

"I'm sure I have no idea," dismissed Portion. "Although you might ask Stilts. He thought he was hiding in the hall when I left your room."

Lord Turville had taken tea with his wife. His strategy in leaving his office for a time was functionally and philosophically identical to those who, upon encountering a seemingly insurmountable problem, close their eyes and hope it'll go away.

Alas, the dictaphone was still gone. However there were signs that someone had been in his office in his absence. The door was ajar, for example, and the safe — the one from which Lady Turville's necklace had been taken a day prior — was eight clicks off.

It was Lord Turville's unbroken routine, upon closing a safe, to turn the dial a fixed number of digits from first position. The fixed number for this week was twenty-three. The object of the practice was to provide for the possibility of opening the safe in complete darkness by listening to and counting the clicks. The fact that he had never been called upon to do this and in no eventuality ever would be presented, to Lord Turville's disciplined mind, no bar to the wisdom of the exercise.

The habit also had the side effect, however, of standing as a quick and handy indicator that someone had opened the safe, or at the very least had tried to. This struck Lord Turville as odd for two reasons — firstly, he had changed the combination and nobody, at all, had the new one. Secondly, there was nothing in the safe. The necklace and Stickle formula had both been stolen, he thought incorrectly, by Algernon Brookbridge.

On opening the safe, though, and inspecting the contents, Topsy realised that these two curiosities were insignificant compared to the third — there was a necklace in the safe; a beautiful diamond necklace.

CHAPTER TWELVE

*In which Teddy follows several lines of enquiry, Algy follows the
odds, and Stilts follows the flow, wherever it may go.*

"That is a very beautiful diamond necklace," appraised Teddy. "Who
put it there?"

In fact, Lord Turville had asked Teddy to join him in his office to
pose that very question.

"I thought you might have an idea."

"Well, clearly this can only be Lady Woolpit's necklace." Teddy
leaned over the desk whereon the necklace was arrayed on a display
cushion improvised from an antimacassar over a nest of business
correspondence.

"This was my thinking as well." Topsy nodded gravely. "What
can it mean?"

"Could precious stones be migratory?" suggested Teddy. "Is it
some sort of involuntary rotation scheme? We have a system rather
like that in London for chaps' top hats. I say we — it's mainly me
that sneaks into the cloak room before the final act to switch about
the hat check tickets."

The necklace scintillated in the crisp winter afternoon light from
the window. It was composed of organic branches in the art nouveau
style, weaving and interweaving and sprouting at seemingly random
and yet mathematically methodical junctions into little diamond
buds, and in this manner ascending from a single wellspring in the
form of a simple perfect prism of stone, embedded in a mellifluous
magma of white gold.

"I've asked Midgeham to fetch the Woolpits." In anticipation of
which, Lord Turville began laying down a thick, protective coating
of pipe smoke. "Perhaps they'll have some idea how their necklace
got into my safe."

"Before they arrive, Tops," Teddy discreetly opened the window and subtly waved it like a flag of truce, "have you any idea how Lady Woolpit knew about Stickle?"

"Have I any idea..." coughed Topsy. "I asked you that. You said that she was some sort of gossip shaman."

"I just wanted to change the subject." Teddy raised the diamond necklace by a delicate branch and let it twist and twinkle. "It's since become interesting."

"Why?"

"Turns out that Bobo heard about it from Stilts..."

"Bobo?" Topsy bent his brow to the name. "Who is Bobo?"

"Beauregard Pilewright." Teddy spoke distractedly as she held the necklace up against the sunlight. "But call him Bobo. He much prefers it. He won't admit it — he might even wince and ask you not to call him that, but he really loves it. In any case, Bobo heard about Stickle from Stilts..."

"Tilden Stollery."

"Excellent, Tops." Teddy held the necklace to her neck and tried to see her reflection in the glazing of a framed photograph of Glitz, wearing a silver festoon and matching tiara. "Yes. Stilts told Bobo about Stickle, and Stilts heard about it from Major Lonegrave, known to you as Major Lonegrave."

"Where did he learn of it?"

"Not from you?"

"No. I barely know the man."

"Didn't you buy a cursed emerald from him?" asked Teddy.

"A what?"

"The Spirit of Myawaddy," explained Teddy, now wearing the diamond necklace. "The centrepiece of Glitz's beastly design. It's meant to be unlucky."

"Oh, right, yes, I suppose I did." Topsy nodded at the memories manifest in pipe smoke. "Although it was Stitch Stollery that handled the actual transaction. Never mentioned anything about a curse."

"Well, he wouldn't, would he?"

"I mean to say, I don't believe in such things, of course, but it would rather explain a lot, wouldn't it? Poor thing."

"It's not the stone itself that's unlucky, Topsy," corrected Teddy, now trying to catch her reflection in the French window. "It confers bad luck on whomever steals it."

"I didn't steal it, though. Paid rather a lot for it, in point of fact."

"You could be just independently unlucky," said Teddy. "It's been known to happen."

"Speaking of which, have you found my dictaphone?"

"I've been a little busy, Topsy," offered Teddy in her defence, as she modelled the diamond necklace in profile.

"Doing what?"

"Well, as you've asked, I've been looking for the Stickle formula."

"I thought Algernon Brookbridge had it."

"I know you did," Teddy reminded him. "You were misled."

"Doesn't matter who has it," puffed Topsy. "Just so long as Brookbridge doesn't."

"I rather think it does matter, Tops." Teddy looked about the office. "Don't you have a mirror?"

"Why does it matter?"

"Just want to see if it suits me." Teddy squinted at her reflection in an ink bottle. "In case Lady Woolpit doesn't want it back."

"I was referring to the formula. Why does it matter who has it, if it's not Brookbridge?"

"Well, clearly, Topsy, Algernon Brookbridge isn't the only person here this weekend whose jinks are higher than the national average."

"To whom do you refer?"

"Well, you, first out of the gate." As a matter of quality control, Teddy danced a short but rigorous Charleston. The necklace held on admirably, and even joined in at the jay-bird. "You tricked Algy into nicking the formula."

"And he expanded the mandate to include Gladdy's necklace," added Topsy, again, erroneously, but they weren't to know that.

"Bringing us back to you, Topsy — you invited people who'd been present during the Woolpit robbery to provide Algy with cover." In the interests of thoroughness, Teddy now performed a quick shimmy and, indeed, at the conclusion of the experiment, the necklace hung down her back.

"It struck me a good idea."

"To fill the house with criminal suspects."

"Well, now, to be fair, Teddy, you were going to be here already," contested Topsy. "I felt that one or two more would only put Algernon that much more at his ease."

"But now someone's taken your dictating machine and, for some reason, put Lady Woolpit's necklace in your safe."

"Sir Oswald and Lady Woolpit, Your Lordship." Midgeham had appeared at the door.

Greetings were made and Midgeham slipped away on the tides of duty, and Sir Oswald and Lady Dora and Lord Turville and Teddy stood smiling at one another over the desk.

"How can we be of assistance, Tommy?" asked Sir Oswald.

Teddy and Topsy shared a curious glance.

"I have a question, if I might," interjected Teddy. "Do you recall who told you about Stickle?"

"Yes," replied Sir Oswald on a tick. "Dora."

"I mean to say, who told you both," clarified Teddy. "From whom did you learn about Stickle, Lady Dora?"

Lady Dora continued smiling vacantly and, as time passed as it inexorably does, she began to blink vacantly as well.

"I can't recall," she finally said.

"You don't know who told you about Stickle?" doubted Topsy.

"Was it you?" asked Lady Dora.

"It was not," replied Topsy with cool suspicion.

"We didn't tell anyone else, Tommy," Oswald assured him with the complaisant confidence of a man who doesn't know that he's lying.

"It's no matter. What I really wanted to discuss was this most extraordinary development." His Lordship introduced Teddy and her glistening neck.

"It's lovely," gushed Lady Dora. "Is it a gift for Gladdy?"

"Eh? No — it's your necklace, isn't it? The one that was stolen."

Oswald and Dora regarded each other with a curious glance that Teddy read as conspiratorial, as though they were briefly considering claiming the treasure.

But in the next moment Dora said, "I've never seen that necklace before in my life."

❦

"The tangled bine-stems scored the sky
Like strings of broken lyres,
And all mankind that haunted nigh
Oh, what ho, Tedds
Had sought their household fires."

Stilts was reading most of this — all but the part addressed to Teddy — from a rowboat on the moat, drifting past Teddy's balcony.

He was wearing a hunting cape and his deerstalker cap and he looked like nothing more than he did a mast of tweed rigging.

"What are you doing, Stilts?"

"Practising," replied the oarsman.

"Your Thomas Hardy?"

"Rowing." Stilts made a sort of 'voilà' gesture at the surrounding context of boat and moat. "The poetry is just for polish."

"But you're not rowing, Stilts," Teddy pointed out as she climbed onto the balustrade, such that her feet were dangling over the water.

"Ah, no, I'm not," agreed Stilts. "I lost hold of the oars, I'm afraid. I'm waiting for them to catch up, but the current is very slow on this stretch."

"That's the problem with moats." Teddy nodded and looked both ways for approaching oars. "It's why you see so few of them with waterwheels."

"I say, that's true, isn't it?" Stilts had to twist to see Teddy as his boat turned slowly to face the opposite bank. "You want to hear some more Thomas Hardy in the meantime? There's this cracking one about a bird on a winter's night…

I leant upon a coppice gate,
When frost was spectre-grey,
And winter's dregs made desolate
The weakening eye of day.

There's more — rather a lot, actually — but that's all I've been able to retain since losing the oars."

"When was that?"

"What time is it now?"

"Coming up on five, I think."

"Ah, then…" Stilts looked about for some sort of natural timepiece. "I still don't know. Could it be an hour?"

"Maybe," acknowledged Teddy. "When were you in my room?"

"Hmm?"

"I said, when was it that you were here in my room?"

"I don't recall being in your room, Teddy." Stilts affected to scan the horizon for signs of oars.

"I'll just ask Aunty Azalea when it was," said Teddy. "She'll remember."

"Will she?"

"She was hiding in the wardrobe."

"I see." Stilts meditated on this for a moment before settling on what he felt was the essence of the argument. "Why was she doing that?"

"She's in training." Teddy cast an eye back into her room. "It's been a childhood dream of hers to join Submarine Corps."

"Oh, right. Jolly good." Stilts' boat now rotated slowly the other way. "Oh, dash it, Teddy, that bounder Brookbridge was in your room while you weren't there. It's hardly cricket, is it, sneaking into your room to plant missives under pillows and whatnot and not giving another chap a fair pop, as it were."

"So you snuck in to remove the offending letter."

"I most certainly did not." Stilts raised his chin indignantly. "That is to say, yes, I did. I didn't find any letter."

"What did you find, Stilts?"

Stilts leaned forward and scanned the area before speaking in low tones, "You know perfectly well what I found, Theodora Quillfeather."

"I need it back, Stilts. Urgently."

"Well, you're not getting it back." Stilts folded his arms resolutely and assumed a noble bearing, like an underappreciated steeple that's found a cause. "I know what you're up to, Teddy."

"No, you don't."

"I do." Once again Stilts tried and failed to create a zone of confidence from a boat turning slowly in a moat beneath a balcony. "You as good as told me so yourself — you said that Algy Brookbridge was leverage against your father."

"And so he is."

"And you're going to give him the formula for Stickle unless your father agrees to let you live your life as you choose to live it."

"If you only knew how absurd..." Teddy stopped for a moment to muse upon a passing cloud. "You know, were it not for a number of other factors, that would be a workable strategy. But that's not what I'm doing."

"You're right it's not, young lady, because I'm sticking to that formula..." Stilts struggled for a more poetic or at least less obvious analogy, but he knew as he spoke that the die had been cast, "...like glue."

"Just hear me out, Stilts..." began Teddy with, unfortunately, the tone she most often employs when she says 'Just hear me out...'.

"Please don't, Teddy." Stilts checked her with a raised hand and averted gaze, but the turning of the boat undermined the effect and in short course he was once again facing forward. "You forget, I know you. I remember when you tried to convince me that the barmaid at the Criterion was Anastasia Romanova."

"What do you mean, tried?" piqued Teddy. "You offered to spirit her to America."

"Well, now I'm immune to your deceptions."

"That works out well, Stilts, because this time I'm telling you the truth."

"Ha."

"I am."

Stilts scrutinised his old London playmate with a cynical squint, undermined only a shade by the brim of his deerstalker. Then the squint broke and his eyebrows took flight.

"I say — did you say that your aunt was in the wardrobe when I was in your room?"

"I did say that, yes."

"I looked in the wardrobe," remembered Stilts. "It was empty."

"I didn't say she was in my wardrobe," said Teddy. "It's a big house, well supplied with quality wardrobes in which to sit. Aunty Azalea's very partial to a Queen Anne mahogany number in the north-east receiving parlour."

"Teddy, you ought to be ashamed of yourself."

"Why?" wondered Teddy. "You're the one who fell for it. Come along, Stilts — I thought you were meant to enchant me this weekend. Do you imagine a girl can ever possibly love a chap who comes between her and her glue formula?"

"Perhaps not." Stilts turned his face to the infinite horizon, like a proud man wronged. "But a gentleman rises above these things to do what's right. You may not love me for it, Teddy, but I mean to protect you from your own worst impulses. If your father or Lord Turville wish to know what's become of the formula you may tell them I have it, and whatever is said or done against my good name I shall bear with dignity."

This speech, stirring as it was, wobbled a bit at the end as Tuxedo Bird hove slowly into view around the north-east corner, standing easily and idly on an oar. This distraction afforded Teddy a crucial few seconds of developmental reflection.

"I suppose that could be made to work." Teddy put a hand to her chin and nodded absently at the approaching penguin.

"What could be made to work?"

"You keeping hold of the formula," explained Teddy. "Although it's going to complicate things when you speak to my father."

"Speak to your father?" queried Stilts in a slightly higher register. "When will I be speaking to your father?"

"Rather soon, I should think. You should know, Stilts, he doesn't like you very much."

"Why ever not?" Stilts took his eyes briefly off the penguin and the oar as they approached.

"I suppose it's not so much that he doesn't like you, but that he'd prefer I marry someone more like Algy or Bobo. Someone with whom he can see eye-to-eye."

"By which he means someone a foot or two closer to average height," interpreted Stilts with the tired cynicism of the frequently tall.

"And you're holding his formula hostage. He'll probably like you even less, now."

"I'm doing nothing of the sort," Stilts sopranoed. "I'm keeping you from holding the formula hostage."

"I don't suppose it matters much which of us has it when I tell Papa that he'll get the formula back when he consents to our marriage."

"Our…" Stilts sat stunned, such that Tuxedo Bird gave him an indulgent honk as he floated past on the oar. "Our what?"

"That's why I had the formula, obviously," Teddy barefaced. "So that I could make Papa give you a chance."

"Oh. Right. I say. Well," articulated Stilts. "I see."

"It's obviously not going to make him like you any better," continued Teddy along baldly audacious lines, "but he might come to respect you."

"Does your father not respect me now?" asked Stilts with little conviction.

"He thinks you're a waster who spends all his time at the track."

"How the devil does that make a chap a waster?" objected Stilts. "Did you tell him that I all but ruined two touts last year?"

"You can tell him yourself," suggested Teddy. "If you think it will help."

Stilts didn't think it would help. He struggled, in the circumstances, to think of anything that would. He watched his oar carry Tuxedo Bird out of sight around the north-west corner of Hardy Hall, and then he thought of something that might help.

"I say, Tedds, what if it was you who had the formula, as it were, when you put the whole thing to your father."

"How do you mean, Stilts?" Teddy spoke with the wondering awe of a child trying to come to terms with the root causes of war.

"I mean to say, what with everything and whatnot, as it were, the whole proposition might be better received coming from you, if you follow my thinking, and you were to be in actual possession of the formula."

A rogue breeze accompanied this and the prow of Stilts' vessel broke free of the opposite bank and turned slowly in unseens currents.

"If you think that's best, Stilts," Teddy acquiesced.

"I do." Stilts had to raise the volume a bit now, as his boat was floating away on the path previously taken by Tuxedo Bird and the oar. "I'll bring it round just as soon as I'm back on shore."

"Plenty of time, Stilts," called Teddy.

❧

There was little time.

Algy felt once again the now familiar but never commonplace urgency of being where he ought not be and, somewhere, someone was reciting poetry.

He inched to the balcony doors and peered between the curtains and over the balcony, one floor above the moat. Below, on the water, was a rowboat, without oars, floating freely, carrying and twirling Stilts Stollery who, for whatever reason, was reading *The Darkling Thrush* by Thomas Hardy out loud.

This meant, at the very least, that Stilts wouldn't be coming back to his room for some little time, and some little time was exactly what Algy needed to find The Spirit of Myawaddy. The process of elimination had worked its inscrutable magic and delivered Algy a clear line of enquiry — Beauregard Pilewright didn't have the necklace and neither did Major Lonegrave. The Turvilles obviously didn't take it and the Woolpits, having themselves recently been victims of a jewellery theft, were above suspicion. The staff of Hardy Hall won't have taken it for the simple reason that if they were so inclined they'd have done so before now. Teddy, the otherwise consummate suspect, was the very person extorting Algy to acquire the necklace, so she couldn't have it. Algy had forgotten about Aunty Azalea but, had he not, he would have eliminated her for sentimental reasons. That left Tilden Stollery, and brought Algy to search his room.

Algy applied once again the tried and found wanting practice of thinking like his prey. Stilts Stollery was a chap, and so was Algy, putting him ahead of the game already. He had just now discovered that Stilts was fond of poetry, as was Algy, putting him further in the lead and feeling just the way he imagined the lone Kalahari hunter feels when taking a bead on the elusive oryx.

Algy stood in Stilts' reception room, being a chap and liking poetry and fully channelling his quarry, and the best he could do was wonder if the The Spirit of Myawaddy might be hidden in a poetry book. There were no poetry books in evidence, in the reception and the bedroom, and Algy's mind was, once again, a blank.

It was only when Algy's eyes settled on a hat stand from which dangled a top hat (which Algy searched, fruitlessly) that he considered the key characteristic distinguishing him from Tilden Stollery — Stilts was abnormally tall. Ironically, this led Algy to search the very place he himself would have hidden the necklace, if he'd had it. Stepping up on a studded leather ottoman, Algy peered onto the top of the wardrobe, where he found his own metal lockbox.

CHAPTER THIRTEEN

In which Algy shares a revelation with Teddy, and Teddy shares a hunch with the Woolpits.

"I couldn't find the necklace, Teddy," announced Algy, "but you'll be interested to know that I've worked out who took it."

Teddy and Algy were meeting in the centre of the trapezoid yew maze on Hardy Holm. This was Algy's idea, communicated by sealed note via Midgeham, with a view to preventing Portion from seeing them together.

"So have I worked out who took it, Algy — you did." Teddy raised the volume because, despite the earlier generalisation that they were 'in the centre' of the maze they were, in fact, lost, and separated by a hedge wall.

"What? I didn't take the necklace." Algy stage whispered, as one does when one wants to be heard and not heard at the same time. "What makes you think I took it?"

"Didn't you?"

"Well, of course not. What would I do with it?" This was followed by a scrambling and shaking of conifer branches. "Where the devil are you?"

"Right here. You really didn't take the necklace?"

"Again, Teddy, I'd be very grateful to learn why it is that you think I did."

"You'll admit you took the formula for Stickle."

"I have already done so," acknowledged Algy stiffly.

"The necklace went missing at the same time," explained Teddy. "It stands to reason that the same person took both the formula and the necklace."

"Impeccable logic, Teddy, but I didn't. I left the safe open, though. Doubtless the real thief profited from that state of affairs."

"I'll remind you, Algy, that whether or not you took the necklace, you're still a real thief."

"Very well, the other thief." Again there was a shuffling of branches, a gentle cascading sound, and a somewhat hard to transliterate "Arf. Oh, well, pish."

"Something wrong, Algy?" asked Teddy.

"I tried to push through the wall and got a hedge-load of snow down my back."

"Right, I'll find you," suggested Teddy. "I'll follow your voice."

"Oh, right oh. What would you like to hear? Thomas Hardy?"

"Tell me who you think took the necklace." Teddy headed, she thought, north.

"Really, Teddy, it's rather obvious when you think of it."

"Speak up." Teddy's voice came to him from a vaguely south-easterly direction.

"I say, it's clear who took the necklace…" Algy stage-shouted loud enough to catch a frog in his throat, "…the only person who would."

"And who is that?"

"Lady Turville."

"Glitz."

"None other," coughed Algy. "It was hideous. She knew it, everybody knew it, except Lord Turville."

"He knew it."

"Did he?" wondered Algy on a north-westerly wind. "Well, she didn't know he knew it, so her plan was to get rid of it, chuck it in the moat, probably, and then claim the insurance and get something nice in its place. Really, Tedds, I'm surprised you didn't think of this yourself."

"There was no insurance." Teddy came upon a set of footprints. "Algy, where are you?"

"No idea."

"You're not moving, are you?"

"I'm looking for you."

"The key requirement to locating a chap by the sound of his voice," explained Teddy, "is that said chap remain stationary."

"Oh, right."

"Now, stay where you are, I'll follow your tracks in the snow."

"Right oh," agreed Algy. "What do you mean, there was no insurance?"

"I mean exactly that, and in any case the Turvilles aren't the sort of people to commit insurance fraud."

"No insurance?" ghasted the prudent Brookbridge. "Of course."

"Of course what?"

"It explains the presence of Tilden Stollery — oh, hi Teddy." Algy greeted Teddy as she popped around a corner.

"What is it that you think Stilts has to do with the missing necklace?"

"Again, rather obvious once you put him together with the lack of insurance and, as you say, the moral rectitude of the Turvilles," said Algy. "He's going to sell it on for her. His family's in the trade, you understand."

Teddy led them back the way she'd come. "And you think Stilts is going to resell The Spirit of Myawaddy for Glitz and replace it with something nice."

"It's the only explanation that makes sense," said Algy. "I've eliminated all other suspects and, you should know, recovered the formula for Stickle."

"I know. It took an age to get Stilts ashore," recalled Teddy with cool despair. "Eventually I had to send out Tuxedo Bird with a tow rope."

"Sshh!" Algy sounded as though he'd sprung a small leak, and then spoke in real whispers. "We're not alone." He gestured at tracks in the snow leading across their path and disappearing around a corner. "There are four of them."

"Algy, those are woozle tracks."

"What's a woozle?"

"We are," explained Teddy. "Those are our tracks."

"So they are." Algy took notice of a difference between shoe sizes which was unlikely to occur between any two random people, never mind four. "Blimey. What's that?"

"What?"

"That avalanche of ice around your neck."

Teddy glanced down as though only then noticing that she was wearing the diamond necklace that had appeared in Lord Turville's safe.

"This bangle? I found it in a box of Christmas ornaments that Midgeham was throwing away. You don't recognise it?"

"I can't imagine I'd forget something like that." Algy furrowed his brow at the glitter. "But, Teddy, if you've got a boggling great bauble like that, what did you want with Lady Turville's necklace?"

"Actually, Algy, I was trying to recover it for Lady Glitz."

"Well, that will no longer be necessary," Algy assured her. "She'll only have been playing along with trying to get it back to keep His Lordship safely in the dark. So, you were really going to give me the formula if I'd got the necklace back for you."

"I said I would."

"But, why, is what I'm wondering," wondered Algy. "Won't your father be a bit spicy about it?"

"I'm sure he was going to turn it over to your father, eventually," claimed Teddy. "He probably just thought he was keeping it a secret from the general public."

"Oh, right, well, you can assure him from me — that particular horse has bolted and made a clean job of it. Do you know that Major Lonegrave knew about Stickle?"

"I'm unsurprised."

"Mind you, he thought it was an abrasive."

"Did he now?" queried Teddy. "I take it he learned this from the Woolpits."

"He did... as it happens." Algy was now jumping in place to try to see over the walls of the maze. "How... did you... know that?"

"Just a hunch."

❦

"What is a hunch, exactly, Teddy, dear?" asked Lady Woolpit.

Teddy had escaped the yew maze in the nick of cocktail hour and arranged for Midgeham to tell the Woolpits that drinks would be taken in the west ground floor loom room. Teddy had just enough time to switch out her maze-navigating outfit for a shimmery shimmy with matching clutch purse, and get started on a pitcher of gin, lemon, champagne, and ice, for her own interpretation of the all-purpose cocktail called the French 75.

"A hunch is all the rage in the States these days," interjected Sir Oswald Woolpit. "It's a sort of combination of high tea and lunch, typically served twice a day, at least on the east coast, and composed mainly of pancakes."

"And you've had one of these hunches, Teddy?" asked Lady Dora. "Was it very nice?"

"Delightful," reported Teddy as she agitated her pitcher with a glass wizzle wand. "We couldn't get maple syrup, though, so we

158

used Creme de Cassis. I also had a notion that Major Lonegrave heard about Stickle from you, Lady Dora."

"Stickle?" queried Dora. "You mean Lord Turville's revolutionary abrasive?"

"Not an abrasive," corrected Oswald, "An emulsive. Stickle is a very powerful mollifying agent, with additional assuasive properties."

"I see." Teddy nodded tentatively.

"Little difficult to explain to the layman," acknowledged Sir Oswald, "but it's very useful in shipping and in the manufacture of fertilisers, that type of thing."

"And how did you come to learn of Stickle, Sir Oswald?" asked Teddy.

The Woolpits, who had presented for cocktails in matching velveteen burgundy tuxedo and evening gown, such that they resembled one immense boot brush, shared a confused glance.

"Come along," urged Teddy. "It was very clear to me that you were being something other than frank when you told Topsy and me that you couldn't recall."

"Why, we learned it from you, Teddy." Lady Dora spoke with wide-eyed solicitude. "Don't you remember?"

There's a very wise axiom that advises to always tell the truth, so that one need only remember one version of it. Of course, Teddy would never and couldn't ever abide by such a prohibition, but in that moment she could just about see the sense of it. It was her who had told the Woolpits about Stickle, last summer, during a village fête at the family furlongs, Chipping Chase Wold.

Lady Dora had on that occasion observed Teddy's Aunty Azalea behaving oddly — not oddly for Aunty Azalea, but she was disguised as the back half of a horse and was standing by it, even though the front half had abandoned her or failed to report for duty. An experienced gossip knows the market potential of a case of nerves in her immediate social circle, and Dora had begun an intense investigation. Partially to distract her but mainly because it was funny, Teddy told Lady Dora, in strictest confidence, about a secret substance called Stickle. She'd thought of the name, first, and then matched it to a legend — Stickle was a powerful amusive, or laughing gas. It was being developed by Teddy's father and Lord Turville for the military, who intended to use it to quickly and tickly bring a peaceful end to any new flare-ups of trench warfare. The individual dressed as half a horse was a government agent who had been exposed to the merest scent of Stickle.

The rest was soundly grounded speculation — Lady Dora had told her husband and Sir Oswald had translated Stickle from an amusive to an emulsive which was in turn reported to Major Lonegrave as an abrasive. When Lady Woolpit went on the air Teddy's father heard the word 'Stickle' and liked it for the new product in which he was investing, and Stickle became an adhesive. Teddy had named Stickle without even knowing that it existed.

"Oh, Stickle," dramatised Teddy. "Quite right. I was thinking of Spickle, a cucumber preservative that Lord Turville was working on last year. Worked a treat but it made the cucumbers taste exactly like Wapping. Stickle, of course you know, is not that."

"No indeed," provided Sir Oswald for the benefit of his far less scientifically-minded wife. "It's a demulcifyer, mainly."

"How do you come to know so much about it, Sir Oswald?" Teddy handed over a glass of French 75 and took the opportunity to close the space and ranks. "It's meant to be top secret."

"One hears things." Sir Oswald tapped his ear knowingly.

"Well, you're right." Teddy passed a glass along to Lady Dora and formed a scrum. "You mustn't let this go any further..." Teddy glanced about the empty room. "...London County Council is buying all the Stickle that Papa and Lord Turville can produce."

"Whatever for?" asked Lady Dora.

"Obviously, my dear, the city is planning to employ Stickle to remove centuries of coal residue from the buildings and bridges of London," explained Sir Oswald patiently.

"Yes," said Teddy. "Yes, that's exactly what they're doing."

"Evening, Woolpits, Miss Quillfeather." Major Lonegrave marched through the door, smartly outfitted in black evening jacket and bow tie over khaki shorts. "The butler told me you were doing cocktails here this evening."

"Midgeham, as usual, is bang on target." Teddy raised her pitcher and a fresh glass. "French 75? Freshly loaded and only fired once."

Lonegrave held up a firm demurring fly whisk. "Never got used to those overly-complicated continental concoctions. Can you do me a Guhawati wati?"

"Ehm. Maybe. What's in it?" Teddy surveyed the cocktail factory.

"Scotch, lemon juice, bitters, and water from the banks of the Brahmaputra River."

"Fresh out of bitters," said Teddy. "How about a simple gin and tonic?"

"Dust the rim with kala namak and you have a Phulabani Pani." The major took notice of Teddy's diamond necklace. "Great galloping Ganapati, where did that come from?"

"It belongs to the char woman." Teddy handed over a deficient Phulabani Pani. "She's letting me wear it while she does the drains. Have you ever seen anything quite like it?"

"I once saw the aurora borealis," reflected Lonegrave. "That's the closest I can think of, for the moment."

"How interesting Major." Portion had slipped in beneath the radar. She was dressed for the library, including thick glasses and low, logical footwear. "Perhaps you can advise me — I'm thinking of moving to the North Pole. Is it true that there are almost no

Brookbridges and that the density of false friends is even less than that of the Orkneys?"

"Hard to say, scientifically, but I'd think it likely, yes."

"Excellent. Thank you, Miss Quillfeather." Portion accepted a conoid of French 75 from Teddy, but her eyes lingered on the river of diamonds.

"Like it?" asked Teddy.

"A gift from Mister Brookbridge?" Portion sniped.

"In a manner of speaking. I took it from him to stop him wearing it to the Oxford rugby annual reunion match." Teddy leaned forward to add, confidentially, "He was going to wear it with sequins. Men are so blind sometimes, don't you find?"

"How very droll, Miss Quillfeather." Portion, having fired off what she felt was a deciding shot at the waterline, floated off, with a vague plan to affect casual conversation with the Woolpits.

She managed it just in time, too. Algy fumbled through the door, preoccupied amidships of his evening suit. The buttons of his waistcoat presented as a Chinese puzzle more confounding than the yew maze because he had, and had yet to realise that he had, put it on the wrong way round and upside down.

"This isn't right, is it?" He sought Teddy's sartorial expertise but then, spotting Portion ostentatiously taking no notice, he gave the confused hem of his waistcoat a snappy tug and accepted a French 75. He was about to dash off a quip by Shelley when Beauregard Pilewright went off behind him.

"What marvel is this?" Beau stared in stunned stupor at Teddy's diamond arborescence. *"T'is constant as the northern star, of whose true fixed and resting quality there is no fellow in the firmament."*

"Eh?" Algy said it but it was a generally held sentiment.

"It's from *Julius Caesar,*" translated Teddy. "He means 'Blimey, would you look at that.'"

"Yes." Beau nodded absently. "Yes, I believe I have indeed taken a liberty with *The Tragedy of Julius Caesar.* I was inspired by the constellation — it's so fetching, Theodora, that it's very nearly worthy of the neck that wears it."

That's exactly the sort of thing that Algy would have said, if he was the sort to say that sort of thing. Instead, he side-eyed Beauregard as he would an opposing fly-half endeavouring to influence play from an off-side position.

"It's nice, isn't it?" agreed Teddy. "Amazing what you can pick up at a church jumble. I got this and a home-baked ginger cobnut for three shillings six."

Beau accepted a French 75 and wry-eyed Algy right back with a dubious disdain cast at what he thought might be a cummerbund of daring design. Then he shot the hem of his own gold brocade waistcoat, which matched his bowtie, and smoothed the lapels of his swallow-tailed theatre jacket.

Teddy set about composing a fresh pitcher as Stilts Stollery ducked into the room, also nattily dressed in black morning coat, grey waistcoat, tie, and trousers, and no socks. Stilts had covered for the absence of socks by wearing canvas espadrilles with a tropical motif in place of dress shoes. The effect was mixed.

As Stilts received his gin brassy he winked at Teddy with all the elan of a man biting into a lemon.

He compounded the effect by leaning in and whispering, "I've cabled ahead and reserved us an hour at the Milton Street registry office. We can be married at ten o'clock, Tuesday morning." Then he stepped back and orb-eyed the necklace. "I say, Tedds, crackerjack of a knickknack, that."

"Thanks." Teddy looked down at the wonder. "I made it myself out of ginger beer wire and garter clips."

Stilts raised an appraising eyebrow. "Platinum alloy chandelier setting, four little nicely formed eight carats, two perfect twelves, and one brilliant cut twenty-four. Worth approximately…" Stilts consulted the ceiling, "…a whack."

"But, whose is it?" Lady Turville pitched this poser. She and Lord Topsy were the last to arrive in time for Stilts' exacting evaluation. They had been delayed while Glitz decided between her replica royal wedding jewellery and black satin evening gown with the depiction of the milky way embroidered in cultured pearl. Pressed by Topsy, who had already measured and remeasured his bow tie and aligned his cufflinks, she settled on both.

"The necklace is yours, presumably," presumed Teddy. "It was in your safe."

"But, who put it there?" wondered Glitz.

"Drifter?" suggested Teddy. "Speaking of your safe, Tops…" Teddy withdrew a black cotton sack from her clutch purse. "We should probably get this back in the vault." She removed the necklace and slinked it into the sack.

"Is that my sock?" Stilts asked, because he was a gentleman, but it was very obviously his sock.

"I needed a jewellery pouch," explained Teddy. "This is the closest I could find."

"Why did you take both of them?"

"Well, I could hardly leave you with just the one sock, could I?" Teddy clipped the jewellery sock into her clutch bag.

"No, right, fair enough."

Midgeham materialised to announce, "Dinner is served." Cocktails were dispatched and the party dispersed.

"We'll have to skip the soup, Topsy." Teddy hooked her arm into her host's. "You don't think I'm taking responsibility for this thing for the rest of the night, do you?"

❦

164

When they found themselves alone in the winter evening darkness of his office, Lord Turville spoke in conspiratorial tones. "What's it all about, Teddy?"

"A jewel heist," replied Teddy in normal, non-conspiratorial tones.

"Yes, I'm aware of that, Theodora. I mean to say, why is it so urgent that we secure the necklace?"

"Once again, Topsy, a jewel heist." Teddy withdrew the sock from her purse. "Another jewel heist is going to be attempted, and it wouldn't be of much use if the necklace wasn't there to be nicked, would it?"

"Ehm. No," agreed Topsy, with inadequate knowledge of that to which he was agreeing. Nevertheless he opened the safe.

Teddy put the sock in it and closed the door. "Now you just need to change the combination."

"I already changed it," said Topsy.

"Not since someone put the diamond necklace in it," pointed out Teddy. "Whoever did that, obviously, can open the safe."

"Yes, there's that, isn't there?" Topsy mused on this for a moment. "But we don't know how whoever it was knew the combination. There's little point in changing it until we know that — we should use a different safe."

"But we do know, Topsy." Teddy indicated that which was conspicuous in its absence. "The dictaphone. It was running when you changed the combination the last time. It recorded the clicks which, as you've observed, are loud enough to open the safe in the dark. Then someone noted the starting position of dial, took the machine, and transcribed the combination by counting the clicks backwards."

"Of course."

"That obviously can't happen now, and nobody's watching your reflection as you turn the dial — you're the only one who'll know the combination."

"So, we hide here and wait for him to try once again to open the safe?" inferred Topsy. "And get him to give back the dictaphone."

"No, Topsy," differed Teddy. "We're dealing with a complex and multi-layered, multi-playered plot. Whoever took your dictaphone also put the necklace in the safe and this player, obviously, has no further need of either. But there are other cold, bold players. We must be canny, Topsy, cleverer than the entire conspiracy — with nuance and nonchalance, we must go and have dinner."

"Oh. Right oh."

"Don't forget to change the combination, Tops."

While Teddy waited beyond the closed office door, Lord Turville performed the combination-changing ritual, including turning the dial twenty-three clicks to the left.

❧

Dinner went well, from almost every perspective. Over the soup, Portion fired off a very neat one comparing the insubstantial and transparent nature of consomé to certain people she could mention although, in a caveat that she begged be expressed to the cook, this broth was comparatively honest.

Beau offhanded a very fitting quote *("Let me have men about me that are fat")* over the broiled goose and another, slightly forced tribute to Lord Turville's toast *("which gives men stomach to digest his words with better appetite"),* both from *Julius Caesar,* as chance would have it.

Algernon thought he'd performed well in the role of the indifferently urbane but, later in the evening, he would have to admit to himself that he had laughed at one or two things that weren't intended to be funny and nodded sagely at many things that were.

Stilts, magnanimous in triumph, was solicitous to his former rivals in love, much in the tradition of Saladin's victories in Jerusalem. He lauded Beau's pointed and salient references from

Julius Caesar and he helped Algy untangle his fish fork from his cufflink.

Major Lonegrave recounted a story of losing a valuable talisman in a rigged game of Crown and Anchor, and Sir Oswald translated it to his wife as a tale of misplacing a rabbit at the Victoria and Albert.

Teddy chatted chirpily and dined daintily but mainly sat in stark reminder to all present that a fortune in diamonds was locked in Lord Turville's safe.

Dinner devolved to brandy and roasted almonds, and the party diffused itself to the games room and library and then further to the south-east receiving parlour and north-east upper floor whist salon.

The Turvilles and the Woolpits shared nightcaps of warm rum in the north-west brass and china gallery and then Topsy and Glitz retired to their room. Lady Turville claimed to have a headache, and she did, but she was disingenuous about its cause.

It was ten-thirty when Lord Turville returned to his office with, uncharacteristically for him, no specific reason for doing so. If he were asked by someone who could compel him to answer frankly — his mother, for probably the only viable example — he'd have admitted that he hoped to find that his dictaphone had been returned.

It wasn't. The office was dark but for a glimmer of winter moonlight shimmering off the snow in the courtyard. It was enough illumination, though, for Topsy to note the one single thing that had changed since he was last in his office — the dial of the safe had been moved fully fifteen clicks to the right. Someone had opened — or tried to open — the safe.

It was the work of a moment to determine which it was. The diamond necklace was gone.

CHAPTER FOURTEEN

Which sullies once again the reputation of the noble drifter.

"But how was it done?" Topsy wanted to know. He and Teddy were in the drawing room, just outside Lord Turville's office. A night sky the colour of irk had curtained off the moon for maintenance and the courtyard was now black and blustery.

"You're quite sure you changed the combination?" asked Teddy. "And that you were alone at the time? You didn't notice any bystanders or a cine camera loitering about the office?"

"It's simply not possible."

"No, I know. It wasn't possible the first two times, either," Teddy sympathised.

Midgeham entered the drawing room as the locomotive force behind a coffee trolley.

"The guests have been informed that coffee is served, Your Lordship."

And, as though on a tether attached to Midgeham, the resident guest list of Hardy Hall trailed into the drawing room. Each displayed something on a scale from pique to curiosity, except Stilts, who smiled like a navvy in a warm bath and had done so since Teddy agreed to marry him earlier that day. Aunty Azalea and Tuxedo Bird had not made an appearance, but only Teddy noticed.

There had been an incomplete wardrobe rotation since dinner. Some — again, notably Stilts — had remained in evening wear. The Woolpits had changed into their matching alpine-themed nightshirts and caps, and Lady Turville was in a dressing gown with a simple brooch tulip on one lapel and corresponding brooch bee on the other.

"What's all this then, Turville?" asked Major Lonegrave, who still wore his dinner jacket and bow tie but had changed to flannel pyjama plus-fours with a camouflage pattern.

"Ah, well..." Lord Turville considered this. His Lordship is a seasoned public speaker and famous for his structured speeches in the House of Lords. His opening address of the recent post-Christmas session had been compared by *The Times* to 'something by Brunel' which, unsurprisingly to his intimates, His Lordship took as a compliment. Normally, however, he likes a little lead time before presenting any ideas bigger than observations of prevailing weather conditions, typically a week or two, and so now found himself saying, 'Ah, well...'

"There's been a jewel heist," announced Teddy. "The diamond necklace I was wearing earlier is no longer in Topsy's safe."

"And you suspect one of us?" ghasted Sir Oswald.

"Why, of course not," fumbled Topsy. "It was doubtless..." He cast an eye over the assemblage, all of whom were bouncing fleeting glances of suspicion off one another. "It was doubtless a drifter."

"Ah, yes, of course." Sir Oswald nodded knowingly. "Same thing happened to us, you know."

"You all might as well know that this isn't the first jewel heist this weekend," added Teddy. "Lady Turville's emerald necklace — The Spirit of Myawaddy — was stolen two nights ago."

"Another drifter?" marvelled Lady Dora.

"Must be some sort of gang," explained her husband.

"Yes, this is what we suspect," agreed Topsy. "Nevertheless, it would be tremendously helpful if you could all recall where you were between dinner and ten-thirty, to help us secure the premises and determine how the theft occurred."

"How did it occur, when it comes to that?" asked Beauregard Pilewright. "Was the safe not locked?"

"Yes," replied Lord Turville. "Yes, the safe was securely locked. We don't know how the, ehm, the drifter managed to open it. There are all manner of possibilities; recording devices, mirrors, smoke, that sort of thing."

Coffee was distributed and brandy added and a convivial, siege-mentality took hold of the room. The wind whistled a song of winter night and jostled the frame of the French doors, further reinforcing the illusion of a wooden cabin in the northern reaches, isolated in the wilderness and surrounded for miles by deep snow and darkened woods and marauding drifters.

A full accounting would read, quite literally, like a police report, and indeed it's more efficient to inventory those who weren't alone at some point after dinner; Midgeham. The butler had been with the rest of the below stairs staff, as he described it, 'fraternising'. There's nothing wrong with a butler learning the Shimmy but he felt the detail to be extraneous to the immediate discussion.

"Right then, there's not much more we can do tonight, I shouldn't think, Topsy," concluded Teddy. "We've done all that can be expected of us until the police are called tomorrow."

"The police?" Glitz all but shrieked. "Surely we don't need to bother the police. That nice Constable Mildminder was here only last month to explain our duty of care for the bothies. We can hardly make him come out again so soon."

"Can't be helped, Gladdy," said Topsy. "The best thing for us all to do now is return to our rooms and get a good night's sleep."

Which, while true, was not in complete correspondence with everyone's plans for the night ahead.

❦

The key to a successful heist is timing.

The wind skirled beyond the walls and a clock struck two within. A hinge squeaked. A floorboard creaked. Beneath the wind did someone speak in whispers.

"That's two o'clock." Sir Oswald said to his wife adding, for he knew that timing was key, "Time to go."

Accordingly, the Woolpits were already suited up in matching midnight black jumpers and jodhpurs and stockinged feet. Sir Oswald opened the door and peered into the north hall, upper floor. It was dark and empty and, but for the howling wind and echo of the second chime, silent.

At that very same instant, Beauregard Pilewright was peeking through his keyhole and determining that the east hall, upper floor, was also free of bystanders. He, too, knew that timing was key, but he was shaky on the importance of wardrobe, and hence was suited for stealth in black silk pyjamas with cobalt piping.

Equally or more unsure of the standards demanded by the league of professional prowlers, Stilts Stollery knocked off his black silk top hat as he slid his head out his door for a preliminary butcher's at the east hall, ground floor. Reasoning that if black was the recommended colour scheme, more black must be more recommended, and he was wearing a tuxedo, cummerbund, black tie, black silk scarf, and patent leather shoes, and no socks. He recovered his hat and determined that the hall was empty.

Portion Beanfield, who had done some early journeyman work with Teddy in London, knew the vital nature of timing and she also had a strong, intuitive notion of what the smart set wears when burglarising stately homes. She had packed poorly, though, and had to settle for a pink quilted dressing gown over pink pyjamas. She wore her ugliest, most effective specs, though, and could see clearly from her door that the west hall, upper floor, was hers to roam unseen.

Major Lonegrave wore a pith helmet, utility vest with flashlight, coconut hammer, and compass, safari jacket, waterproof tent-canvas trousers, and swamp boots, as he allowed his eyes to adjust to the darkness of the north hall, ground floor, and listened to the peal of the second chime fade into the warble of the winter wind. He surveyed the terrain and he sniffed the air. He removed a shooting glove to touch bare fingertips to the floorboards to feel for the subtle vibrations of the footfall of the wily, nocturnal galago.

Satisfied that, in the narrow definition of the term within the English country house, he was the apex predator, Major Lonegrave set out on the trail of his prey.

Moving in a clockwise fashion through the house, up and down stairs, and around corners, the prowlers encountered only empty halls. The instant that Stilts turned the corner from the east hall, ground floor, into the north hall, Major Lonegrave disappeared up the stairs. As the major silently padded out of the north hall, upper floor, Portion Beanfield entered it, and so on.

Consequently, they all arrived at their destinations simultaneously and equally unseen.

Stilts cautiously entered the room and closed the door behind him and then, looking straight ahead, was startled by who he saw, but nowhere near as startled as was he who saw him.

Portion, tragically underestimating the volume of the swoosh and swish of even the finest quilted dressing gowns, was unaware that she had been rumbled before she even closed the door. She squealed in shock and disappointment as she found herself seized from behind.

The Woolpits fared much better. They had achieved their destination and were, in one sense, alone. In another, far more pertinent sense, they were overwhelmed.

Beau, though he arrived at his destination entirely unobserved, carried himself, as always, as though all eyes were on him. He took a moment to shoot his cuffs and stretch out an errant pleat at the waist of his dressing gown before opening the door, glancing both ways, and slipping in. He maintained his level sang-froid throughout, right up to the moment when he was grabbed by the ankles and swept into the air.

Even over the wind, Portion's squeal, Beau's boing, and even Tuxedo Bird's sentimental honk all carried moment and meaning to the keen ear of Major Lonegrave. He listened and he deciphered, and he understood. He nodded and pursed his lips and generally expressed the quiet satisfaction of a man who knows his business. He opened the door of the Woolpits' room, stepped inside, and softly closed it behind him.

"Hello, Major," spoke the figure at the balcony window, black in silhouette but for a glistening diamond necklace.

🐨

"I take it you've come looking for this," asked Teddy. "Still want it?"

"I... I don't know." Lonegrave removed his pith helmet to consider this puzzler.

Teddy slinked like the black leopard of the Kakamega to the drinks cabinet and clicked on a brass bar lamp.

"You don't," Teddy assured him. "Shall I explain why?"

"If you wouldn't mind, terribly."

"Brandy?" Teddy poured two snifters.

"If there's no Chuwarak."

Teddy handed over a snifter and took a leather odeon chair by the balcony doors, beyond which the wind rushed and hushed and whistled through the balustrades and the trees on Hardy Holm.

"You stole The Spirit of Myawaddy." Teddy spoke flatly, like a professor introducing a lecture she's given more times than she can recall.

"I did."

"Twice." Teddy held up two illustrative fingers.

"Also correct." The major assumed another odeon chair, such that he and Teddy each had their own floor-to-ceiling balcony window to frame them.

"But you never stole the Woolpits' necklace," continued Teddy. "Because it was never stolen."

"I paid them good money for it," confirmed Lonegrave. "And the rupee was quite weak against the pound, at the time."

"They gave it to you before the shooting weekend, which is why nobody who was there — not even Algernon Brookbridge — recognises it."

"Presumably so."

"You bought this necklace so that you could give it to Lady Turville in exchange for The Spirit of Myawaddy," said Teddy. "Then you cadged an invitation here this weekend, on the pretext of being interested in investing in Stickle, even though Lord Turville told you months ago that there was no room for new investors."

"I soon realised that she wouldn't sell it — she'd designed that atrocity herself, and she somehow adored it like an only child."

"No, she didn't, actually," corrected Teddy. "But I can see how you might have got that impression — she didn't want Lord Topsy to know that she'd spent a minor fortune on a boondoggle."

"Amounts to the same thing."

"It does," agreed Teddy. "But then, somehow, you stumbled upon the open safe."

"Wilderness instincts." Lonegrave nodded into the past and drew on his brandy. "I heard someone sneaking about, and followed him down to Lord Turville's office. I hid while he opened the safe and, amazingly, left the necklace behind. So I just took it."

"But why didn't you replace it with the diamond necklace while you had the chance?" asked Teddy.

"Didn't have it with me," recalled Lonegrave. "I went back to my room to get it, but by the time I did, some madwoman was haunting the halls."

"She's not mad, just shy."

"Well, I couldn't get past her. Tried to wait her out. Fell asleep. By the next morning it was too late."

"So you came up with the dictaphone trick," guessed Teddy.

"I didn't, in fact," admitted the major. "Happened to be talking with His Lordship about this Stickle business when he accidentally recorded our conversation. He turned off the device, and then asked for a moment alone to change the combination of his safe. I turned it back on as I left."

"So you were able to return that night and put the diamond necklace in the safe," said Teddy. "Thusly completing the transaction and not, technically, stealing The Spirit of Myawaddy, which you believe would have only made the curse worse."

"Assuming that's possible."

"And now you're free to return the emerald to Burma, finally breaking the curse."

Major Lonegrave nodded and allowed himself another sip of brandy, in that moment as curative as the finest Chuwarak or Chaang. "How did you work it out?"

"Well, above all, Major, you were clearly not telling the truth when you said that you believed the curse to be already broken," barristered Teddy. "You said yourself that the bad luck lingered on with those who'd handled the thing. Furthermore, you managed a score of negative thirty-seven playing billiards against yourself."

"That was, for me, a comparatively good result."

"And by all accounts, unless a drifter actually took Lady Dora's diamonds, no one could have," said Teddy. "The Woolpits must have been involved. It stands to reason that they sold it to someone. It wasn't Algernon Brookbridge, because if he had any of his own money he'd have used it long ago to marry Portion Beanfield. It wasn't Beauregard Pilewright because he's a swindler, not a thief. You're the only one who could have and would have paid cash for the necklace, and because you told them your plans for it they knew they could get away with also making a claim against the insurance, which is what the police suspected from the start."

"You know about the insurance fraud, too?" marvelled the major.

"Bobo Pilewright told me they had no money," recounted Teddy, "but then, after the robbery, they tried to buy into Stickle."

"Dashed lucky for them they happened to have insurance."

"Not luck, exactly, Major," Teddy clarified. "Bobo sold them the only policy underwritten by an insurance cooperative that he established for the specific purpose of going bankrupt."

"Why would he do that?"

"That's his business niche." Teddy drained her snifter conclusively. "He sells his wealthy friends shares in guaranteed sinkers but he doesn't actually invest the capital. Then, when the insurance cooperative or musical comedy or riverboat casino or thriving new residential community of Thamesmead disappears in a puff of broke, he just keeps the money."

"Then the Woolpits must have confided in Pilewright." Lonegrave spoke as one, having witnessed all of mankind's failings up close, has still yet managed to find one more.

"They conspired with him." Teddy refilled their snifters. "I've little doubt that it was his idea."

"And then the bounders — they stole it last night. I've paid them for it, they've collected on the insurance, and then they took the dashed thing back."

"No, they didn't." Teddy sipped her brandy and gazed at the swirl of night beyond the balcony doors. "I did."

"You did? But, how did you crack the combination?"

"I didn't," said Teddy. "I put a decoy sock in the safe before Topsy locked it and changed the combination. The necklace remained in my purse the entire time, but I needed him to be convinced that it had really been stolen; his talent for live performance is very modern, you see — Lord Turville needs to actually believe in his lines. I needed everyone — most particularly you, Major — to think that the necklace was in the wind and that if you were going to recover it you needed to do so before the police were called in the morning."

"I was taking it back for Lady Turville, you understand," insisted the major. "It belongs to her, now."

"I know, Major," Teddy assured him. "All you wanted was to return The Spirit of Myawaddy to Burma without having to steal it, so that you can end the curse. And that meant giving Lady Turville something of equal or greater value."

"Just so." The major brooded over his brandy until, it seemed, it reminded him of a point of order. "Where are the Woolpits, if it comes to that?"

"Searching Bobo's room," answered Teddy with flat certainty.

"Eh? Why?"

"They think he took the necklace," said Teddy. "It stands to reason — he's a crook, he knows that the necklace is technically between owners at the moment, and someone told them that he took it."

❦

"Have we duly considered the possibility that this Azalea woman is simply mad?"

This inspiration entered Sir Oswald's head while it was inside a steamer trunk in Beauregard Pilewright's room. Initially, the Woolpits had been what they thought was delicate and discreet, but as they realised that Beau was not, as expected, sleeping in the next room, and that he had no fewer than three steamer trunks, four hat boxes, a boot box, and a brass and leather grooming kit, and that they were all in a state of disorder from Algy's earlier efforts to find a necklace among them, the search became, in a word, frenzied.

Lady Dora peered at her husband from out of the wardrobe, across a receiving room floor of tailored suits and fitted shirts and hand-polished collar studs.

"It only stands to reason that Beauregard took it," she deduced. "He's a crook, and he's the only one who knows that my necklace is, technically, between owners."

"We've run out of places to look," protested Oswald.

"Obviously we haven't, dear," pointed out Lady Dora. "It must be here somewhere."

"But what if he comes back?"

It was an unlikely contingency, for at the moment Beauregard Pilewright was suspended by his ankles in Major Lonegrave's sitting room.

The major had set the trap after finding Algnernon Brookbridge in his room. Normally, he'd have used braided vines looped through a sturdy joint of an old-growth Pyinkado tree, primed with a sapling bent to a sixty degree angle, forming a powerful spring. As it was, he'd had to make do with knotted sheets pullied through the chandelier and tied to a heavy ottoman hanging over the balcony. He'd have been very pleased and not a little surprised to see how well his improvisation had performed.

Beauregard was less pleased. After trying and failing to free himself, he'd resigned the time remaining until he was inevitably discovered to the development and refinement of a cover story. The truth was that he had come looking for The Spirit of Myawaddy. When he'd seen Lady Woolpit's necklace on Teddy, he'd worked it all out in an instant, and had concluded that Lady Turville's necklace must be in the major's room. He'd further deduced that the emerald was fair game — what was the major going to do, call the police? Finally, that strange woman who'd been hiding behind the rhododendron in the music room had hinted very vividly that Major Lonegrave had The Spirit of Myawaddy in his room.

All that, however, would make a very poor explanation for how he'd finished up suspended by his ankles in Major Lonegrave's sitting room.

The wind piped a frozen aria around Hardy Hall and kicked up frozen flakes from the grounds and skittered them against the windows.

Tuxedo Bird watched this from Teddy's room, his beak against the glass, a melancholy throbbing somewhere in his tiny penguin heart. The fact is, Tuxedo Bird had been born in NW1 and had never been nearer the Antarctic than a school outing once to Putney, but the call of the frozen south pole is innate and universal to his kind, in much the fashion and degree that Goodwood calls to a chap every year after he reaches the age of majority, and the weather made him homesick for his friends and family at the zoo.

Then, as though in answer to this inexpressible yearning, a figure appeared, reflected in the glass and framed by a soft, grey glow from the hall, and looking just like home.

Stilts, wearing full evening dress, top hat, and patent leather shoes, appeared to Tuxedo Bird like a fair compromise — rather than all the friends he had left behind, here was one immense friend. He hopped from foot-to-foot and flapped his wings and Stilts, charmed to all distraction, did the same, and forgot why he had come to Teddy's room.

He would later remember that his intention had been, once again, to save Teddy from her own kleptocratic instincts, by stealing back the diamond necklace and returning it, in a manner he had yet to calculate, to Lord Turville's safe.

"You!"

By which Algy meant Portion. Algy was not, by nature, a suspicious man nor, for that matter, particularly attentive, but events of the last two days had stirred in him a heretofore untapped vigilance. He had taken the precaution of hiding the Stickle formula more cleverly — under the bed, wrapped in a pillowcase — and had taken to sleeping on the divan by the door, which he left unlocked as a means of lulling any intruders into a false sense of security.

Sure enough, his expectations had been met to a nicety when, just after two o'clock in the morning, the handle of his door gently, slowly, quietly turned, and the door opened. From awareness to action was but a flash. Algy selected his signature move, the dump tackle, which involves wrapping his arms around his opponent's hips, raising him in the air, and then giving him over to gravity. Where any intruder built to standards would have had hips, however, this one appeared to have shoulders, and Algy found himself hugging Portion from behind and saying, 'You!'

Portion reserved her comments to "Auugh!"

"Portion, why would you want to steal the formula?" wondered Algy.

"What formula?" wondered Portion right back at him. "I came to steal the necklace."

"But I haven't any necklace," pointed out Algy, reasoning further, "and if I did, I would just give it to you."

"Would you, Algy?" swooned Portion.

"Of course. Why did you think I had a necklace?"

"I thought it was you who'd taken the diamond necklace from Lord Turville's safe," said Portion. "I was going to give it back to him, before you got in trouble."

Algy, finally releasing Portion, asked, "Why would you think that I'd taken it?"

"Who else would be so daring and clever?" Portion wanted to know. "In any case, an old woman hiding in my wardrobe said you'd done it."

"Well, I didn't." Algy, taking up and holding a position by the drinks cabinet, poised a brandy bottle for action. "Did this old woman say why I'd nicked the necklace?"

"No…" reflected Portion. "I assumed it was so that we could afford to marry. You said that you had a daring plan."

"So I do have a daring plan." Algy poured two modest, two o'clock brandies. "But it's nothing to do with stealing necklaces."

"I should have known better." Portion accepted a snifter but her eyes lingered on those of Algy. "I'm sorry I misjudged you. I'm sorry about everything."

"Nothing of the kind, Port old sport. For you, I'd steal the Mona Lisa." They drank to this proposal. "Just say the word."

❦

"Where is The Spirit of Myawaddy?" Teddy asked the major. "I'm sure you knew better than to hide it in your room."

"London. Sent it out with the post the morning after I took it." Lonegrave glanced up from his brandy as though it had just whispered something pertinent. "If that young *badirchand* wasn't after the Spirit of Myawaddy, why did he open the safe?"

"He wanted something else that was in it," said Teddy in ode to the obvious. "The formula for Stickle. He's going to give it to his father who, in exchange, will accede to Algy's marriage to his sweetheart."

"Should have taken the necklace, too, to cover his tracks," advised the major.

"Or at least closed the safe," agreed Teddy. "Algy's not a natural schemer. For him, the height of subterfuge is the spinning lateral pass."

"But surely he's the first chap His Lordship suspected."

"Absolutely," confirmed Teddy. "The only one who doesn't know how obvious it is that Algy took the formula is Algy — he was meant to take it, you see, as part of a plan to oblige his father to meet the terms of an original agreement. Speaking of which, Major, I'm going to need you to return the dictaphone."

"Ah." Lonegrave nodded at his brandy. "Not so easily done, I'm afraid."

"It's not in London too, surely," doubted Teddy.

"No, not in London," Major Lonegrave looked gravely out at the cold night and whipping wind. "I chucked it into the moat."

CHAPTER FIFTEEN

In which Jimmy Elbows has his day.

When Teddy came down for breakfast only Lady Turville was already in the breakfast room, constructing a precarious stratification of bacon, kippers, fried soda bread, roasted ham, and toast and jam. The sun was twinkling off the frosted trees and grounds of Hardy Holm and whelming through the high windows in columns. And yet nothing scintillated like Glitz's tillow of diamonds, though her easy smile was a close second. This morning, she wore no other jewellery.

"Good morning, Teddy." Glitz posed with her plate in one hand and cutlery in the other, framing the treasure. "Look what I found in my room this morning."

"Kippers?" Teddy poured a cup of coffee.

"No, Teddy, the necklace." Glitz squeezed into place across from Teddy, such that they were both framed by a window and a distance from the door. "Tom says it's mine to keep, and we don't have to call the police."

"I have even better news, Glitz." Teddy leaned over her coffee and lowered her voice. "The Spirit of Myawaddy is on its way home to Burma."

"Does Tom know?" whispered Glitz.

"Topsy has other worries, for the moment."

"Has it anything to do with Sir Oswald and Lady Dora?" Torn between a passion for scuttlebut and a passion for soda bread fried in bacon fat, Glitz ate with her fingers.

"Tangentially. Why?"

"They left this morning, very early." Glitz accompanied this announcement with a crispy kipper. "So did Major Lonegrave, and Beauregard Pilewright."

"How very odd."

"And Midgeham tells me they left their rooms in a disgraceful state." Glitz munched a scandalised slice of toast. "There's an ottoman on the ice outside the major's window."

"Ice?"

"The moat froze over during the night."

"Of course."

"It's tied to some knotted sheets," continued Glitz. "What could he possibly have been doing?"

"Setting a trap for jewel thieves?"

"Be serious, Teddy. I think the man might be touched."

"He just believes himself to be unlucky." Teddy drank a silent toast to the major. "He'll be better soon."

"Now, Teddy…" Glitz, with a discreet glance at the door, withdrew an envelope from the pocket of her dressing gown. "I have received a letter from your mother."

"I can only imagine." Teddy topped up her coffee from the pot and her strength of will from a headstrong daughter's reserves. "Best hand it over."

"It says…" Glitz started to say, but in that moment Stilts stumbled into the breakfast room.

"What ho, ladies." Stilts was still wearing his tuxedo and patent leather shoes, although they were somewhat twisted and hiked, and his top hat was missing, and he was staring at Lady Turville's necklace. "Why, Your Ladyship — you're the jewel thief?"

"It's her necklace, Stilts." Teddy poured him a hot cup of black necessity. "What have you been up to?"

"I passed much of the night with your penguin." Stilts fell into place next to Teddy and took up the cup. "He's a very matey bird. Did you know the moat had frozen over? You wouldn't believe the marvels a penguin can perform on ice. And we built a snowman, of a sort. More of a snow mound, really, but he seemed very happy with the result."

"Where is he now?" Teddy asked this distractedly as she scanned her mother's letter.

"Sleeping it off in my room," said Stilts. "We welcomed sunrise with champagne and caviar. I say we — he had the caviar, I managed the other bit."

"Were you celebrating something, too, Tilden?" asked Glitz.

Stilts winked clumsily at Teddy over his coffee. "I should say so, Lady Turville."

"Good morning, Hardy Hall." Portion Beanfield appeared at the door, just short of singing her lines. She was wearing sunshine yellow scarves and sweaters and skirts, flat shoes, and her thickest specs. "What a glorious, sunshiney morning. Hello Stilts, you're looking very dapper. I'll bet all the chaps will be going without socks this season. Good morning, Lady Turville, what a lovely lot of lustrous loot you have on." She poured herself a cup of coffee and hopped up into a chair. "Teddy, my best friend and fiend. I take it you had a tranquil night, given the place is still standing."

"What ho, Ports," welcomed Teddy. "Is all forgiven?"

"I should ask you that," said Portion. "I'm sorry I ever distrusted you, Tedds. And even sorrier I accused Algy. He's as loyal as a sheepdog."

"Algy?" Glitz queried with ham.

"Algernon Brookbridge," sang Portion. "Algy and I are going to be married."

"Algernon Brookbridge?" Glitz seized on what she felt was the overlooked subtext of the headline. "What about your young man in London?"

"Algy is Portion's young man in London," explained Teddy. "She came here this weekend to keep him honest."

"To be near him," corrected Portion. "I trust him more than I trust my own eyes."

"You burned most of his letters," Teddy reminded her, "and exiled the rest."

"I told him how sorry I was, and he stayed up all last night rewriting them," marvelled Portion. "He has ever such a good memory."

The object of adored affection came through the door at that moment, wearing a woolly expression and dressing gown.

"Last two." Algy laid two small envelopes on the table before his bride. "The one in which I rewrote *The Lady of Shalott* with a happy ending, and the list I made when you went to the chemist's for me that time I was stung by a bee."

"What ho, Algy," hailed Teddy.

"What ho, Tedds. Morning all." Algy appeared to notice in that moment that this best of all possible worlds was full of people and other delights. "Is that bacon?"

"I understand that you and Miss Beanfield are to be married," said Glitz, with the tone of one trying to make sense of a world gone mad.

"Congratulations, Algy." Stilts toasted the couple with his coffee cup. "I hope you'll be very happy, Portion."

"Yes, I…" Algy froze in the moment, a slice of ham suspended over his plate. In stark testament to his essential innocence, he had only just then realised that he was standing at a precipice, and that Teddy held the fanged adder, for he had little talent for metaphor. She could and doubtless shortly would expose him as the master thief who had spirited away the formula for Stickle. "Yes, I certainly hope so."

"Algy must first gain his father's agreement," Teddy explained to Lady Gladys. "Isn't that right, Algy?"

"Ehm. Yes. Yes, I do."

"But you have that largely sewn up, haven't you?" added Teddy, reassuringly.

"In the main." Algy dubiously entrusted the ham to his plate.

Teddy affected to be distracted by her mother's letter. "If you want my advice, you'll get the formalities sorted straight away, before your father discovers something that causes him to change his mind."

"She's quite right, Algy," agreed Portion. "We should make an appointment with the registry office the moment we're back in London."

"You can have Stilts' appointment," said Teddy with the appearance of sudden inspiration. "Ten o'clock on Tuesday, at the Milton Street registry office."

"Oh, uhm, yes, of course," braved Stilts. "Greater need, and all that, but, well, Teddy, well, dash it, when are we meant to get married?"

"That might have to wait for a bit, Stilton old cheese." Teddy held up the letter. "Did you have cause to write to my mother this weekend?"

"Why, yes, as a matter of fact, I did." Stilts spoke as one modestly confessing to saving orphans from a burning barge. "I had told her that I would keep her abreast of developments here at Hardy Hall, and I thought I would take the opportunity to press my campaign with the home office, as it were."

"Did you tell my mother that you were an atheist?"

"Passionate and practising." Stilts gave a clever little wave of the head. "Lady Dora told me that your whole family feels very strongly on the point."

"Oh, they do," Teddy assured him. "My mother has told me to keep no less than ten miles distance between us."

"Eh?"

"How could you not know that she was deaconess of Saint Barts, Chipping Wold?" asked Teddy. "And was presented to the queen last year in recognition of her tract reconciling *Regula Sancti Benedicti* with off-track betting?"

Stilts stared in stark horror at the words he'd written as they smouldered before him in his mind's eye, as of fire and brimstone. "I assured her that her grandchildren would be raised in the tradition of the Romantics."

"Not Shelley," hoped Algy.

"I put particular emphasis on Shelley," lamented Stilts.

"It'll blow over, in time," consoled Teddy. "I remember, only a couple of years ago, my mother had a falling out with Maude Tadcaster, her oldest friend, over the order of the *Magnificat* during Vespers. This year, at Christmas, Mama allowed Lady Tadcaster's name to be spoken in her presence."

Stilts moaned.

"Buck up, Stilts," encouraged Algy. "You can be witness at our wedding. Won't that be jolly?"

Glitz watched Algy, Portion, and Stilts trail out the door in deeply varying levels of enthusiasm for the project before saying, "I didn't know all that about your mother?"

"All what about my mother?"

"Oh, dear, poor Teddy." Struck by a sad surmise, Glitz lowered her fork. "Beauregard Pilewright has run off, Algernon Brookbridge is marrying Portia Beanfield, and now you're forbidden from having anything to do with Tilden Stollery. None of the bachelors from this weekend are at all eligible."

"Say, that's right." Teddy nodded, expressly baffled by this series of uncanny developments. "Funny how that's worked out."

"At least we're rid of that hideous necklace." Glitz admired her reflection in a butter knife. "And I have this lovely replacement. It's all ending quite happily, after all."

"Not for absolutely everyone," cautioned Teddy and, as though to emphasise the point, Lord Turville entered the second dining room.

He was, uncharacteristically, dressed for comfort, in a tweed, three-piece hunting suit, with the top button of his waistcoat left undone, and a soft collared shirt. He had a sheaf of correspondence in his hand and an air of Sunday morning serenity on his face.

"Good morning, Gladdy, Tedds." He set about the sideboard with an appetite to rival that of his wife.

"Morning, Topsy," greeted Teddy. "You'll be happy to know that Algy is leaving shortly with the formula for Stickle and urgent plans to turn them over to his father."

"He'll be glad to have them, I should imagine." With a fish knife, Topsy flipped a kipper into the air and caught it on his plate.

"You'll be less happy to know that your dictaphone is at the bottom of the moat."

"What a peculiar place for it," Topsy judged it. "Do you know who put it there?"

"Major Lonegrave," replied Teddy. "He took The Spirit of Myawaddy so that he could return it to Burma, thus lifting what he believes is a curse on everyone who's had a hand in stealing it in the first place."

"Curse?" queried Glitz.

"These things can often be self-fulfilling," explained Teddy. "The major thought he was cursed, so he might as well have been. He needed to break the curse by getting the emerald back from you without stealing it, so he bought that marvel..." Teddy nodded at the diamond chaparral around the neck of Lady Turville, "...from the Woolpits. By the nature of the plan, though, he had to do it in secret, a feature the Woolpits employed to also make a claim on their insurance, through a policy provided by Bobo Pilewright."

"Beauregard Pilewright is an insurance salesman?" puzzled Glitz. "I thought he was a financial wizard."

"He's a swindler. He sells shares in enterprises that he knows are going to fail, such as an insurance cooperative that sells only one policy on a diamond necklace that he knows is going to be stolen."

"It's a good job you didn't marry him," observed Glitz.

"Yes, it was a fine run thing, too," agreed Teddy.

"And, now that it's all coming out, I heard that there was a touch of nerve disorder in the family."

"Yes, Bobo's uncle planted money trees around the City. Either that, or he went to prison on behalf of a sweet little old lady," recounted Teddy. "I think the truth is somewhere between the two — his uncle went to prison for hiding the money of sweet little old ladies in untraceable investments throughout the City of London. Just as Bobo did with the proceeds from his jewellery insurance scam."

"Just a minute," Glitz tore her eyes from her mirror-knife, "this is Lady Dora's necklace?"

"No, Glitz, it's your necklace, given to you as payment for your old one," said Teddy. "That's why, when I wore it last night during cocktails, everyone pretended to not recognise it — anyone who'd seen it was involved in the conspiracy. But then, after they thought it had been stolen from Topsy's safe, the Woolpits and Beauregard tried to get it back for themselves."

"Is that why they left without a word?"

"I would think so, yes," said Teddy. "Although in the case of the major it was more likely that he didn't want to have to answer for the dictaphone. He said he'd get you a new one, Tops, but I don't suppose that's much comfort."

"On the contrary, that works out very nicely." Topsy, too, was eating a kipper with his fingers. "Miss Giltspur will be very pleased to know that I'm moving to the latest model, with the timer option, if you wouldn't mind conveying that to the major, Teddy."

"But, what about the contract with Abernathy Brookbridge for Stickle?"

"Mister Brookbridge has signed a new contract." Topsy held up a letter from his little stack. "This is a cable from your father. Yesterday Brookbridge paid off our loan with the bank, and settled new terms with your father, conditional we sign away our remaining rights to Stickle."

"I see."

"Seems the Woolpits are buying into the enterprise, too." Topsy referred back to the cable. "And, curiously, the new terms require us to explicitly resign any claims on the formula being employed to remove coal residue from buildings, bridges, and public monuments."

❦

The key to a successful heist is timing. Putting back that which has been taken, on the other hand, is another matter altogether. Timing enters that equation hardly at all and, in fact, it's in the reverse heist that the policy so unimaginatively employed by Jimmy Elbows becomes conspicuously effective.

It's important to note that Jack 'Daw' MacGraw and Donny 'Noddy' Wandle, both on duty that Tuesday night (Portion and Algy's wedding day), had agreed between them that, in light of the current, buoyant population levels of penguins at the zoo and the universal difficulty in distinguishing one penguin from another, the less said about the incident the previous week the better.

So it was with ambiguous sentiments that they perceived, waddling out of the night-time fog, what appeared to be a penguin, accompanied on the one side by a dapper young flapper in black frock coat and, on the other, another, grotesquely oversized, penguin. As the characters clarified out of a mist inflected with skipping flakes of damp snow, big brother penguin proved to be a tall chap in a tuxedo and top hat, looking very much as though he'd been to a wedding reception at which he'd toasted the happy couple ardently and often.

This oddest of audiences stopped before the security guards. Tuxedo Bird honked happily. Stilts weaved a bit. Teddy smiled and said, "Lovely evening."

"Aye," Daw, assuming the prerogative of seniority, agreed, on behalf of the entire security apparatus of the south gate of London Zoo, that it was a lovely evening.

Having danced around the obvious, conversation waned. Daw and Noddy looked at Tuxedo Bird. Tuxedo Bird looked longingly beyond the gates. Stilts teetered.

"Shall we say five quid each," proposed Stilts, finally.

The security guards regarded one another in silent consultation.

"Go on, then," they agreed in unison.

Negotiations concluded and finalised, Stilts, Teddy, Tuxedo Bird, and Noddy tottered through the zoo to the Antarctic pavilion. Tuxedo Bird fidgeted by the gate while it was opened, then he scampered through and, in his happy, homecoming glee, stamped single-mindedly to the banks of the penguin pool.

But then he stopped as he realised that he waddled alone. He wobbled around and looked back at his weekend society and knew, in his simple, flightless manner, that he couldn't have it both ways — he was home, but Stilts and Teddy weren't. He tilted his head at Stilts, who replied in kind. Then he raised his wing in a wave and Teddy waved back and said, "We'll come and visit soon, Tux."

Then Tuxedo Bird slipped on some ice and fell into the pool.

Teddy Quillfeather Mysteries

I hope you enjoyed this first Teddy Quillfeather mystery. I know I did, and I've been looking forward to saying so for years and years.

I've known Teddy, under various names, for about a decade, during which I've plotted and planned to give voice to this character of quick-witted, kind-hearted, extroverted enthusiasm for living life and taking liberties.

Teddy Quillfeather is a fast-talking, faster-acting flapper, from a fanciful, golden-aged, nineteen-twenty-never, where every country house she visits is host to con artists and swindlers and forgers and crooks. This, happily, is directly in line with Teddy's attitude and aptitude for elaborate counter-plots.

Each Teddy title is a clean, complex, standalone cosy composed of layers of malfeasance and mystery and misdirection. What there isn't, in something of a departure for the genre, is murder. Instead, Teddy takes a turn towards the manor house mystery of manners, to which she brings proactive problem solving that often sees her fully implicated in capers involving smooth swindles and highwire heists, sticky fingers and loaded dice, and dark horses running dodgy courses.

Teddy's personality infuses and drives the narrative but, in another departure, I've very much enjoyed expressing these stories in the third person. I hope that resulted in broader, funnier sequences and insights into the perspective of varying eccentrics, from hard-luck Major Lonegrave to take-it-as-it-comes Tuxedo Bird.

Now, finally, she's out in the world with, if you like her, a series of adventures ahead.

Hardy Haul at Hardy Hall

The first ever Teddy Quillfeather!

The theft of an immensely valuable, immensely ugly necklace is only the beginning of the intrigues and oddities at a country weekend at Hardy Hall where Teddy Quillfeather's mother has sent her with strict instructions to select an eligible bachelor from a shortlist of aristocrats, eccentrics, and egos.

But when Teddy sets out to discourage the suitors and discover the looters with her natural knack for applied shenanigans she instead uncovers countless conspiracies, complicated by country house courtesies. It's a comedy of manners and caper of manors and the only solution, if you're Teddy Quillfeather, is obviously another heist.

Frauds On Favourite

Teddy's at the track and the odds are odder than ever.

Teddy's off to the races in this multi-layered multiplier mystery of dark horses and dodgy courses, pawky jockeys, unstable stables, impossible odds, crooked bookies, and a track-wide conspiracy to deny the punter an even chance. That's more than enough to invite a counter-con from Teddy, but when the family paddock is implicated in race-fixing, she does what she does best when the odds go against her — she raises the stakes.

The next one!

Even as we speak, plots are being planned and teams are being manned for another daring heist, caper, or sting. Fortunately, there's a newsletter with the very latest updates and release dates, plus cryptic clues and custom content and cartoons confined to the club. You can sign up for the combined Boisjoly/Quillfeather Infrequent Newsletter at the link below or by flashing the QR code on your phone.

http://indefensiblepublishing.com/newsletters/

Anty Boisjoly Mysteries

Teddy's cousin Anty Boisjoly is a Wodehousian gadabout, clubman, and gentleman idler with a knack for unravelling the ravelled wrong, which is usually at least two locked-room mysteries with a gallery of eccentric suspects and subtexts, and typically two twists in the tail of the tale.

Each book is a stand-alone, self-contained mystery with a few recurring characters, including Vickers, who has been gentleman's personal gentleman to the Boisjoly gentlemen for three generations, and the wary and weary Inspector Wittersham of the Yard.

The Case of the Canterfell Codicil

The first Anty Boisjoly mystery

In *The Case of the Canterfell Codicil,* Wodehousian gadabout and clubman Anty Boisjoly takes on his first case when his old Oxford chum and coxswain is facing the gallows, accused of the murder of his wealthy uncle. Not one but two locked-room mysteries later, Anty's matching wits and witticisms with a subversive butler, a senile footman, a single-minded detective-inspector, an irascible goat, and the eccentric conventions of the pastoral Sussex countryside to untangle a multi-layered mystery of secret bequests, ancient writs, love triangles, revenge, and a teasing twist in the final paragraph.

The Case of the Ghost of Christmas Morning
The Christmas number
Anty Boisjoly visits Aunty Boisjoly, his reclusive aunt, at her cosy, sixteen-bedroom burrow in snowy Hertfordshire, for a quiet Christmas in dairy country. But even before he arrives, a local war hero has not only been murdered in a most improbable fashion, but hours later he's standing his old friends Christmas drinks at the local. The only clues are footprints in the snow, leading to the only possible culprit — Aunty Boisjoly.

The Tale of the Tenpenny Tontine
The dual duel dilemma
It's another mystifying, manor house murder for bon-vivant and problem-solver Anty Boisjoly, when his clubmate asks him to determine who died first after a duel is fought in a locked room. The untold riches of the Tenpenny Tontine are in the balance, but the stakes only get higher when Anty determines that, duel or not, this was a case of murder.

The Case of the Carnaby Castle Curse
The scary one
The ancient curse of Carnaby Castle has begun taking victims again — either that, or someone's very cleverly done away with the new young bride of the philandering family patriarch, and the chief suspect is none other than Carnaby, London's finest club steward.

Anty Boisjoly's wits and witticisms are tested to their frozen limit as he sifts the superstitions, suspicions, and age-old schisms of the mediaeval Peak District village of Hoy to sort out how it was done before the curse can claim Carnaby himself.

Reckoning at the Riviera Royale
The one with Anty's mum
Anty finally has that awkward 'did you murder my father' conversation with his mother while finding himself in the ticklish position of defending her and an innocent elephant against charges of impossible murder.

If that's not enough, Anty's fallen for the daughter of the mysterious mother-daughter team of gamblers, there's a second impossible murder, and Anty has a very worrying idea who it is that's been cheating the casino.

The Case of the Case of Kilcladdich
Time trickles down on a timeless tipple
Anty Boisjoly travels to the sacred source waters of Glen Glennegie to help decide the fate of his favourite whisky, but an impossible locked room murder is only one of a multitude of mysteries that try Anty's wits and witticisms to their northern limit.

Time trickles down on the traditional tipple as Anty unravels family feuds, ruptured romance, shepherdless sheep, and a series of suspiciously surfacing secrets to sort out who killed whom and how and why and who might be next to die.

Foreboding Foretelling at Ficklehouse Felling
Anty's reddest-of-herringed, twistiest-of-turned, locked-roomiest manor house mystery yet.
It's a classic, manor house, mystery-within-a-locked-room-mystery for Anty Boisjoly, when a death is foretold by a mystic that Anty's sure is a charlatan. But when an impossible murder follows the foretelling, Anty and his old ally and nemesis Inspector Wittersham must sift the connivance, contrivance, misguidance, and reliance on pseudoscience of the mad manor and its oddball inhabitants before the killer strikes again.

Mystery and Malice Aboard RMS Ballast

The pirate number!

Anty, Vickers, Inspector Wittersham, and a passenger list of howling eccentrics find themselves prey to the sway and spray of the Scilly Seas when what at first seems a simple, unexplainable, locked-state-room murder twists into a tale of buried treasure, perilous weather and dangerous endeavours at sea.

Death Reports to a Health Resort

The case of the case of withdrawal

We meet more of Anty's eccentric extended family when he visits his uncle at a retreat for fans of the first deadly sin and enthusiasts of the sixth. Motivated suspects are plump, piqued, and plentiful when the most disliked man in the spa is the victim of a locked room murder, but Inspector Wittersham soon points the finger at Anty's uncle and things only get worse when a second murder occurs that both eye-witnesses — Anty Boisjoly and Ivor Wittersham — swear was impossible.